A Passion for Sauerkraut

The Humble Vegetable for Good Health

Hofer Publishers
Saskatoon, Sask. CANADA

Copyright © 2001 by Samuel Hofer

National Library of Canada Cataloguing in Publication Data

Hofer, Samuel, 1962-
A passion for sauerkraut

ISBN 0-9684268-2-4

1. Sauerkraut. 2. Cookery (Sauerkraut) I. Title.
TP444.S27H63 2001 641.4'6 C2001-910899-0

Recipes compiled and edited by Samuel Hofer
Book designed by Samuel Hofer
Cover photographs by Samuel Hofer
Photo of dish on front cover: Greek-Style Chicken with Sauerkraut

Printed in Canada

Published by:
Hofer Publishers
Box 9784
Saskatoon, Saskatchewan
S7K 7G5
Phone: (306) 242-8162
Fax: (306) 975-9169
Internet: hoferpublishers.com

To Andy and Rita

Contents

Acknowledgments

This cookbook would not have been possible without the many sources of sauerkraut lore available in books and on the World Wide Web, despite the information being quite fragmented. The many online sauerkraut enthusiasts sharing their recipe ideas helped me discover the versatility of sauerkraut. *The Cultured Cabbage,* by Klaus Kaufmann and Annelies Schöneck, provided solid knowledge about the history, science, and health-benefits of lactic acid-fermented vegetables. *Healing With Whole Foods,* by Paul Pitchford, also provided insightful information about raw cultured vegetables. *Home Canning,* published by Alberta Agriculture, was an invaluable guide for making sauerkraut at home. I would like to thank the following people for their help with this work: Sharon Harrington, for finding many fantastic recipes for me to try. Andrew Field, for helping me make my first two batches of sauerkraut. Bernice Friesen, for her help in clarifying certain passages in the introductory material and for her proofreading help.

If cooking with sauerkraut is a new experience for you, I hope that you will soon discover that this humble vegetable provides more goodness than you may have realized. If you're a sauerkraut lover already, may you delight in finding new ways to serve your kraut.

Introduction

Sauerkraut! I love it, and for good reasons. As a recipe ingredient it enhances the flavor and aroma of many different dishes, salads, soups, breads, desserts, and appetizers. As a fermented vegetable it provides many health benefits to the body, as you'll discover soon enough.

Sauerkraut lovers tend to love sauerkraut with a passion, while others, particularly those with krautless ethnic backgrounds, tend to dislike it or view it with disdain. Perhaps it's because they generally find the assertive flavor and aroma of fermented cabbage difficult to embrace or they've never experienced the diversity of cooking with sauerkraut. But as you will discover by trying the recipes in this cookbook, sauerkraut offers a lot more than its name suggests. Whether people eat sauerkraut or not may indeed be a cultural thing, or perhaps it's an acquired taste. Never the less, people who don't eat sauerkraut are missing out on a whole lot of goodness, taste-wise and health-wise. As a food ingredient, sauerkraut is like onions and garlic – it brings pizzazz and health-giving properties to your food.

Three years ago I was looking at some cabbages at a market garden near Blaine Lake, Saskatchewan with my friends Andy and Rita. All three of us expressed our amazement at the huge heads of cabbages displayed there, some of which weighed up to 15 pounds, grown by a woman who came to Saskatchewan from Australia, where Andrew himself emigrated from. Out of the blue Andy suggested that we make sauerkraut that fall. Rita, his wife, remarked in a skeptical voice: "You're going to make sauerkraut?" "Why not?" Andy said. "Sauerkraut is good for you." What's ironic is that Rita has sauerkraut-eating roots (Polish and Ukrainian); and her Ukrainian mom makes the most delicious rice cabbage rolls using sauerkraut leaves. I, myself, having grown up in a Hutterite community often ate sauerkraut, but had completely overlooked this tradition as having great importance. So when Andy suggested that we make sauerkraut, something inside me clicked into place. It seemed like the right thing to do. One could call this a wake-up call or a nudge from Spirit. In an instant I realized what a great idea this was. We decided there and then that we would make sauerkraut that fall.

Shortly after, we had the opportunity to purchase a large used stone crock and a cabbage cutter. Subsequently, we purchased 80 pounds of cabbage from the market garden and one Saturday afternoon in early October began our first batch of sauerkraut. Maybe we got lucky, but this first batch turned out to be possibly the finest sauerkraut we had ever tasted. It even impressed a neighbor who, having Austrian roots, had been making her own sauerkraut for years. My love for kraut has much to do with rediscovering it as an adult, having shown only casual interest in it since leaving home 18 years ago.

Shortly after we made our first batch of sauerkraut I got the idea to write a cookbook featuring sauerkraut recipes. I held back for a year, however, thinking that I'd need a partner ingredient or idea to go along with sauerkraut, just as I had done with two of my other cookbooks, one featuring Soups and Borschts, the other Perogies and Dumplings. Cucumber pickles seemed to be a good partner, but sauerkraut by itself continued to inspire me enough as I consumed my portion of the kraut that my friend and I had made. A year later we made the second batch. It was then that I decided that sauerkraut could stand on its own. The uses for sauerkraut seemed endless. My passion for sauerkraut increased to almost an obsession. While growing up, I experienced sauerkraut served in only three ways. I loved it even then, but not nearly as much as I do now. Sauerkraut was eaten as a basic salad sweetened with sugar (Hutterites like their sugar), as a sweetened stewed vegetable side dish, and the classic sauerkraut with pork sausages. But now I found myself reading about sauerkraut history and the health benefits of cultured foods. Although sauerkraut appeared to be the underdog of the vegetable world, I saw that there was more to this unpretentious food than I had realized. Sometimes we have to rediscover something in order to see the its inherent value. This cookbook is about my rediscovery of the goodness of kraut.

Sauerkraut History and Traditions

Many people assume that sauerkraut was invented by the Germans, but that's a misconception. "Sauerkraut" is merely a southern German and Austrian word, meaning, "sour cabbage". Cabbages were already cultivated in ancient Egypt and Greece. In the second century BC, the Greek philosopher Theophrastus, writing about plants, mentioned three types of cabbage. Dioscurides, a Greek physician, wrote of cabbage, "it is healthier if only warmed, then cooked."

Chinese people ate sauerkraut as far back as the third century BC. Back then, they fermented cabbage in rice wine. During the building of the Great Wall of China more than 2000 years ago, preserved cabbage was a common part of workers' meals. The rice diets of workers were deficient in vitamin C, which is abundant in cabbage.

The practice of fermenting cabbages was carried from the Orient to Eastern Europe by roving tribes of Tartars (members of a group of people inhabiting parts of Europe and Asiatic Russia). In 1485, a cookbook titled "Mastery of the Kitchen," was published in Nuremberg, which contained the first printed recipe for sauerkraut. Sauerkraut's popularity spread throughout Germany and France, especially in the Alsace-Lorraine region.

Before the invention of food preservation, preventing scurvy was a real concern for sailors. They were often at sea for months at a time without any fresh fruits and vegetables. In the eighteenth century, Captain Cook, knowing the benefits of fermented cabbage, carried almost 8,000 pounds of sauerkraut on his ship, which enabled him to sail around the world without losing a single man to scurvy. This brought new awareness to many people about the dietetic importance of sauerkraut.

Fermented foods are popular in different parts of the world. Centuries of travel by explorers took sauerkraut to many countries. The Koreans make *kimchi*, a hot spicy fermented cabbage. Today in China families still make their own *paocai* or *yancai,* the Chinese version of sauerkraut. Fermented cabbage is also popular in Japan and Italy. From France comes the famed *choucroute garni*, a mountain of sauerkraut with pieces of sausages, pork, and ham. In Russia, sauerkraut soup (*shchi*) and cabbage pie (*piróg*) are very popular. Polish people use sauerkraut to make *bigos* (sauerkraut and meat) and *perogies* (stuffed dumplings). And of course, who can resist *Golubtsi* (Ukrainian cabbage rolls) using soured cabbage leaves? Armenians make sauerkraut-bulgur soup. The Dutch eat chicken stuffed with sauerkraut at Christmas as a way to end the year and pork and sauerkraut to start the

New Year. The symbolism associated with this tradition is that a chicken scratches the earth back over the old year and a pig uses its snout to push the earth forward, or to look ahead. Many people in European cultures believe it is good luck to eat sauerkraut, not only for the New Year but at graduations and weddings as well. These are but a few of the kraut foods and traditions from people around the world.

When Europeans immigrated to North America, they brought many of their traditions with them, including their dietary customs. Eastern European immigrants settling in North America ate their favorite Old Country foods three times a week, which of course included their beloved sauerkraut. People would not have survived had they not processing their own foods. Fresh vegetables weren't available year round as they are today. Preserved foods were essential for survival.

As society progresses and becomes more modern, old traditions fade away or lose some of their intrinsic value. With modernization came advances in farming methods and we became more mobile, able to ship food from one country to another quicker. Fresh vegetables and fruits became readily available year round. Unfortunately, most producers, needing to keep up with the growing worldwide marketplace and demands, began supplementing increasingly nutrient deficient soils with artificial fertilizers, as well as using other potent herbicides and pesticides to try to control weeds and insects. But since everything God creates has its built-in capacity to fight for survival, the so-called pests develop immunities, therefore the need for newer and more powerful chemicals increase. Today GMOs (genetically modified foods) are being produced, which in the long run may be a boon or doom, depending on how carefully we learn from them. There are plenty of different points of view about these issues. All of us who value good health should be concerned. Certainly, organic farming is on the increase, and that is good. One doesn't need to be a brain scientist to figure out that our health is directly related to the quality of the food we consume. Isn't it common sense then to look back in time, to old practices and diets, to natural ways of growing and preserving foods, and to supplement our diets with whole foods such as sauerkraut at least once or twice a week?

Fermented foods have been around since ancient times and were indeed a boon to the health of people throughout, even though they likely didn't understand why from the point of view of science. Fermented foods such as sauerkraut, sourdough bread, miso, tempeh, tamari, chutney, yogurt, cultured butter, and cheese, among others, are products widely available today. There appears to be a growing awareness in how beneficial lactic acid-fermented foods are to our health. Why are these foods so good for us? The question requires a two-fold answer. First, fermentation neutralizes unhealthy chemicals found in many

12

raw foods. Second, it adds a host of beneficial microorganisms to food, which make it more digestible and increase the healthy flora in our intestinal tracts.

There are plenty of books on the market that deal in great depth with fermented foods, but as the title of this book promises, I'll focus on sauerkraut, for that's where my passion is due to sauerkraut being such an awesome food for the creation of wonderful, tasty dishes. As is reflected in the recipes of this cookbook, people use sauerkraut in endlessly creative ways. I must point out that this is not a health or cure-all cookbook in the typical sense. It is a cookbook that takes one of the most healthful lactic acid-fermented foods available to us and shows you how to use it in many of your favorite foods. I don't propose to change the world and people's diets as some health cookbooks attempt to do. I am realistic. People don't change their culinary habits that easily. What I hope to accomplish is to make more people aware of this remarkable vegetable.

Would you believe that sauerkraut continues to be second only to mustard as a hot dog topping? Over one billion servings of sauerkraut are consumed each year, with 25 percent of all households buying sauerkraut (about 3 pounds per capita). No sandwich with kraut is more famous than the Reuben – a combination of corned beef, Swiss cheese, sauerkraut, and Russian dressing on rye bread. This sandwich was invented more than 60 years ago by Reuben Kulakofsky, a deli owner in Omaha, Nebraska. While crisp kraut is favored for sandwiches and salads, most cooks favor a long simmering period for other dishes so the kraut becomes tender and absorbs the dish's other flavors. In its most traditional uses, sauerkraut is cooked slowly along with pork ribs, sausages, or pork roasts. It's also a surprise ingredient in chocolate cakes, pies, pizza, breads, and many other foods. So now that you know just a bit more about sauerkraut history and what it can offer, can you see why I was so excited about rediscovering sauerkraut and why I developed such a passion for it?

Health Benefits of Eating Sauerkraut

You may have thought that I was a bit over the edge with my passion for sauerkraut, but that's only part of the story. Great taste is one thing, but once you discover that eating sauerkraut has tremendous health benefits far beyond that of preventing scurvy to sailors long ago, you begin to realize that you have a winner on your hands, albeit an unsung hero of sorts. The key is in the lactic acid, which virtually all fermented foods contain. There are many books on the market containing information on the benefits of lactic acid, and scientists are constantly discovering more and more about how it affects the body.

By definition, sauerkraut is "acidic cabbage," the result of natural fermentation by bacteria indigenous to cabbage in the presence of 2 to 3 percent salt. The fermentation yields lactic acid that, along with other minor products of fermentation, gives sauerkraut its characteristic flavor and texture. When you add salt to cabbage, two things occur: First, it causes an osmotic imbalance resulting in the release of water, sugar, and other nutrients from the cabbage leaves. The expelled fluid is an excellent growth medium for the microorganism involved in the fermentation. Second, the salt concentration inhibits the growth of many spoilage organisms and pathogens.

There are two different forms of lactic acid, superior (L) and inferior (D). The body produces both forms of this acid. When all body processes are functioning properly, the body produces L, but when overstressed and not functioning properly, it produces D, which tends to create health problems if the body doesn't get enough of the superior acid. This is why you need to make sure to get plenty of L acid in your diet. Sauerkraut is one of the best L acid foods available to us. It is fat free and low in calories. One cup of undrained sauerkraut has only 40 calories. It provides almost one-third of the recommended daily allowance for vitamin C, plus it has other important nutrients. Here's a breakdown of the nutrients in a half-cup portion of sauerkraut:

- 20 calories
- 1.1 g protein
- 0.2 g fat
- 3.4 g carbohydrates
- 1.4 g raw fiber
- traces of vitamin A

- 20 mcg vitamin B1
- 20 mcg vitamin B2
- 18 mg vitamin C
- 730 mg sodium
- 490 mg potassium
- 31 mg phosphorus
- 46 mg calcium
- 0.5 mg iron

Consider sauerkraut as being the food that balances your inner ecosystem. Incorporating unpasteurized lactic acid-fermented vegetables into our diet on a daily basis can greatly aid in the recovery and maintenance of digestion. Poor digestion can lead to serious problems such as colon cancer, pancreatitis, and immune system dysfunction. A healthy colon is very acidic and is populated with high numbers of friendly bacteria such as Lactobacillus Acidophilus. These microorganisms feed on the waste left over from our digestion and create lactic acid, which the colon requires to keep healthy. Without beneficial bacteria and the lactic acid they create, the colon does not have enough acidity to stop the growth of harmful parasites and yeasts. With a diet not receiving good amounts of lactic acid foods, the environment in the colon can become hostile even to the acidophilus and other healthful bacteria. The results of such imbalances can lead to Candida Albicans, among other yeasts and parasites. Some effects of Candida are fatigue, poor memory, intense food cravings, gas, loss of sexual desire, bad breath, and indigestion. Candida is also linked to allergies, chronic fatigue syndrome, irritable bowl syndrome, chemical sensitivity disorders, and even cancers.

The good news is that the same types of beneficial microorganisms that create lactic acid in the colon are naturally present in all vegetables. They are especially high in cabbage. What's remarkable about sauerkraut is that in the fermentation of this vegetable, these friendly bacteria increase dramatically while harmful bacteria cannot survive in the acidic environment. It's a win/win situation. The acidic environment fosters the growth of the friendly bacteria, which in turn create more lactic acid. In short, when we eat sauerkraut, we reap the benefits of ingesting an entire ecosystem into our internal ecosystem.

But there's more. Even before the sauerkraut reaches the colon, it produces good effects in the stomach. The stomach naturally secretes hydrochloric acid, which breaks down our food before it moves into the smaller intestine, where absorption of nutrients into the bloodstream begins. Lactic acid in sauerkraut can partially compensate for reduced hydrochloric acid when consumed with a meal. Sauerkraut and other cultured vegetables are essentially already predigested, which means that even before you eat them, the friendly bacteria have already broken down the natural sugars and starches in the vegetables, a job your own saliva and digestive enzymes do for you. By eating sauerkraut, your body is already one step ahead. As we get older, our stomach's secretion of hydrochloric acid decreases, thus it makes tremendous sense for the elderly to supplement their diet with lactic acid through the foods they consume. Another way sauerkraut benefits digestion in the stomach is by assisting the pancreas. The pancreas secretes enzymes essential to digestion into the stomach. You may have guessed it. Sauerkraut is also an excellent source of these enzymes. Cabbage and sauerkraut are like little enzyme powerhouses. They help maintain a body's enzyme reserve and eliminate toxins, rejuvenate the cells, and thus help strengthen the entire immune system. Sauerkraut is like a key that fits neatly into the secretion glands of the stomach – to lock and unlock those glands in accordance with the varying balances of acids and alkalis. It is obvious that good health begins in the gut. Eating food that rejuvenates the inner ecosystem is a wise thing to do.

People sometimes complain that sauerkraut creates flatulence. Because sauerkraut triggers cleansing of the body, a person may initially experience an increase in intestinal gas as wastes and toxins in the intestinal tracts get stirred up for the body to eliminate. Within a short time people notice improvements.

The stimulating and healing effects of sauerkraut and sauerkraut juice:

- encourage the secretory functions of mucous membranes in the mouth
- help treat asthma
- help strengthen the acidity of the stomach
- prevent constipation
- improve blood circulation
- encourage function of the pancreas and stimulates the secretions of all digestive juices
- detoxify the intestines
- stimulate peristaltic movement of the intestines
- support natural resistance against infections
- help treat fever and rheumatic pains
- rid the body of worms and typhoid fever
- help normalize cell respiration
- help cure polyps

- encourage secretory functions of mucous membranes in female genital organs
- help lower the level of sugar in the blood and urine
- help cleanse the blood
- can help increase longevity
- help control the craving for sweets
- help alleviate morning sickness in pregnant women
- can help sufferers of anemia, arteriosclerosis, bronchial asthma, colic, diabetes, gout, hardening of the arteries, headaches, rheumatism, and more
- help re-establish healthy intestinal flora after taking antibiotics

Here are more health-benefits of raw cabbage and sauerkraut:

- cabbage leaf poultices can be applied to the skin to help cure various skin diseases
- cabbage leaves relieve engorgement of the breasts in nursing mothers
- cabbage and sauerkraut contain dithiolethiones, a group of compounds that have anti-cancer and antioxidant properties
- cabbage and sauerkraut contain indoles, substances which protect against breast and colon cancer
- cabbage and sauerkraut contain sulphur, which has antibiotic and antiviral characteristics
- cabbage and its juice can help clear depression
- cabbage and sauerkraut mildly stimulate the liver and other tissues of stagnancy
- raw unsalted sauerkraut helps increase and distribute oxygen in the body

Whether you eat sauerkraut for its good taste or its preventative or curative properties, I think you will agree that it is indeed a food of which you should always have a good supply in your home and consume it on a regular basis. It is a remarkable creation, one that has delighted and helped sustain emperors, explorers, and common folk for thousands of years. Lactic acid-fermented foods, particularly sauerkraut, prove that we can – to use the expression, "have our cake and eat it too" – be well fed and well nourished at the same time. This is a rare combination in this age of processed and synthetic foods. Humble sauerkraut – once a winner, always a winner, as much now as in ancient times. Enjoy the recipes. *Guten Appetit!*

Making Your Own Sauerkraut

Here are precise directions for making sauerkraut. Carefully following these instructions will result in success. Never the less, if you've never made sauerkraut, you might want to start with a small batch. It's much less heartbreaking to throw 20 pounds of spoiled kraut into the compost bin than it is to pitch out 80 pounds. I've heard of even expert kraut makers having a batch go bad. The first and second times my friends and I made kraut, we followed the same directions and had the same results, which is why I emphasize following instructions very carefully.

If possible, purchase the cabbage from mid to late-season crops, as it tends to be juicier then, but don't let that stop you from purchasing cabbages from the store and making sauerkraut in the middle of the winter. Choose large, disease-free, firm, well ripened heads. Cabbage quality differs with the variety and growing conditions. Mature, large headed types, weighing 6 to 15 pounds with a solid, white interior, are the most desired for kraut. Also consider obtaining cabbages that were harvested after the first frost. Although not essential, this makes the cabbages slightly sweeter. The sugar in the sauerkraut is necessary for fermentation to take place. Let the cabbage heads stand at room temperature for a day or two to wilt. This causes the leaves to become less brittle and less likely to break when cutting. Trim the outer leaves and wash the heads. With a large sharp knife, cut the heads in halves or quarters. Remove the core. You can also add the core, finely cut, to the kraut. To cut the kraut, use an ordinary kraut cutting board with the blades set to cut about the thickness of a dime. The setting of the blades may be varied for a very fine or coarse cut, depending on your preference. You can also shred the cabbages using a food processor. Cut each head into wedges and shred in the processor.

Quantities of Salt and Cabbage Needed:

Add 2 teaspoons pickling salt for each pound of shredded cabbage, or 3 ½ tablespoons pickling salt for every 5 pounds of shredded cabbage. Use only pickling salt or sea salt. Sea salt is excellent for lactic acid fermentation because it contains many minerals and trace elements. Never use regular iodized table salt, because iodine can prevent the bacterial fermentation to occur as well as cause discoloration of the kraut. It's worth noting that vegetables grown organically require less salt because of their superior quality. Cabbage is the only vegetable that can be fermented with very little salt or no salt at all. Its leaves are rich in vitamins, minerals, and naturally occurring lactic acid.

Mix the salt and cabbage (in batches of 3 to 5 pounds) in a large enamel or stainless steel pan and let stand for 5 minutes. This waiting period is important, as the salt will begin to draw the juice and sugar from the cut cabbage and the shreds are less likely to break than if they are mixed with the salt and packed at once. Mixing thoroughly is also important to ensure equal distribution of the salt. Uneven distribution of salt can cause spoilage.

      Wash and rinse the inside of your container very well, then sterilize it with boiling water. Pack kraut into container. (Read the information below on how to choose the right container). To pack the cabbage, use a large wooden tamper to force out the air and get the juice flowing. The reason for tamping the kraut, other than drawing out the juices to make a brine, is to eliminate air pockets, which may cause the kraut to spoil.

Adding other Ingredients to the Fermentation Container

You can modulate the flavor of your sauerkraut by adding caraway seeds, dill seeds, juniper berries, bay leaves, peppercorns, cranberries, sour apples, and even some onions and garlic. This will require some experimentation, so it is advised not to add anything other than the pickling salt the first time you make sauerkraut. If you wish to add some of these ingredients, the approximate amounts to add to 20 pounds of cabbage are: 1 ½ cups sliced onions, 4 to 6 bay leaves, 1 ½ to 1 ¾ tablespoons caraway or dill seeds, 2 to 3 tablespoons juniper berries, 3 to 4 apples (sliced), and 1 ½ to 2 cups cranberries. Add all the ingredients or only some of them.

Fermenting Red Cabbage

Although it is not as popular for making sauerkraut, red cabbage can be preserved in the same way as white cabbage. Red cabbage, however, has to be mashed thoroughly, as it is a very hard vegetable, and even heavy tamping may not extract enough juice. To compensate for the lack of juice, add some lactic acid-fermented vegetable juice or water. Generally, caraway or dill seeds, juniper berries, bay leaves, sour apples, and onions are also added. Add these ingredients more or less according to your preference. The approximate amounts to add to 20 pounds of cabbage are: 1 2/3 cups sliced onions, 4 apples sliced, 6 to 8 bay leaves, ½ to 2/3 tablespoon caraway or dill seeds, and 18 to 20 juniper berries.

Low Salt and Salt-Free Sauerkraut

Cabbage can be preserved using very little salt (2 ½ to 3 tablespoons pickling salt or sea salt for 20 pounds of cabbage) or no salt at all. This is good news for people on low-sodium diets. You can also add onions, caraway or dill seeds, some thyme, and juniper berries. For 20 pounds of cabbage, add these ingredients more or less in the same amounts as shown above. In addition, add 5 cups of whey to the kraut, as it is an excellent fermentation supplement. To obtain the whey, place a thin cloth into a strainer and pour warm buttermilk or sour milk into it. The fluid that strains through is whey. Ferment in the same way as kraut to which salt is added.

Containers for Fermenting Sauerkraut

There are various kinds of containers you can use to ferment sauerkraut, such as oak barrels, stone crocks, and food-grade plastic or glass containers. Check your local beer and wine supply store for the latter. The most inexpensive plastic containers are 5-gallon plastic pails used to ship foods such as pie filling, peanut butter, and pickles. You may be able to pick these up at bulk food stores, bakeries, and restaurants just for the asking. Food-grade plastic and glass containers are excellent substitutes for stone crocks. Other 1 to 3-gallon non food-grade plastic containers may be used if lined inside with a clean food-grade plastic bag. But be absolutely careful so that the kraut contacts only food-grade plastics. Do not use garbage bags, trash liners, or plastic buckets not meant for food use.

For anyone making a lot of sauerkraut for commercial use, investing in a large oak barrel may be practical, but for the average person it isn't. My personal preference is to ferment the sauerkraut in stone crocks, which come in various sizes. They are easy to keep clean and if you take good care of your crock it will last you a lifetime. You can find stone crocks at select hardware stores, though you may have to do some searching or asking around. These stores will likely also sell cabbage cutters. If unsuccessful, try the World Wide Web. Also, consider searching in second hand stores, auctions, or the classified ads in newspapers. When I first began making sauerkraut, my friend and I managed to obtain a used stone crock large enough to make 80 pounds of sauerkraut, along with a kraut cutter, for a good price of $80. Not everybody will be that lucky, but that shouldn't be a problem. You can most certainly purchase plastic or glass containers from your local beer and wine supply store; these containers range from 6 to 20 gallons in capacity. Here are some basic quantity guidelines: A 1-gallon container is needed for 5 pounds of cabbage. A 5-gallon container is ideal for fermenting about 25 pounds of shredded cabbage. A 50-pound bag of fresh cabbage makes 16 to 20 quarts of kraut.

Tamp the cabbage into the container until the juice comes to the surface. If you use a large enough container, you can also pack a few full heads of cabbage into the container. These are ideal for making cabbage rolls. Remove the core from the head and put 2 to 3 tablespoons of pickling salt into the cavity; place the cabbages into the crock with the cavity side up. Continue packing the cut cabbage around the heads. Fill the container to no more than 80 percent capacity, as the fermentation will expand the cabbage. Cover the cabbage with a clean white muslin cloth, cheesecloth, uncolored bath towel, or food-grade plastic, then with a weight. You can use an untreated wooden board or dinner plate weighed down with a clean rock or other object (size and weight depending on the size of the container). When using a wooden weight, make sure to use only birch or beech woods. Never use fir or pine. Their strong odors could easily be transferred to the kraut. Another ideal weight to use is a plastic bag partially filled with water. This bag should be heavyweight, absolutely watertight, and intended for use with food. The weight should be such that it forces the juices to come to the bottom of the cover, but not over it. The cloth should be moist but not covered with the juice. The weight needed to keep the juice at the proper height may vary, especially during the first few days of fermentation and with changes in temperature. Check the sauerkraut every 3 or 4 days. If the brine level is too high, remove some of it, or if not, add water. Never add chlorinated water. If you don't have accesses to spring or purified water, make sure to boil the chlorinated water to remove the chlorine. Also remember that you have to add salt to any water you put into the crock after fermentation has started [2 tablespoons salt to every imperial quart (5 cups)]. Always boil this water and add the salt while the water is still hot, making sure the salt dissolves completely.

When I first began researching how to make kraut, I found different suggestions as to what the ideal fermentation temperature should be. Basically, at 70 degrees Fahrenheit, allow about 4 weeks for the fermentation process to be complete, at 65 degrees Fahrenheit about 5 weeks, and 60 degrees Fahrenheit about 6 weeks. Just so you know, if the temperature is kept at 75 to 85 degrees Fahrenheit, fermentation will take place faster and the kraut may be ready in about 2 weeks, but these temperatures are not recommended. Temperatures above 75 degrees Fahrenheit will likely result in premature fermentation and possibly the spoilage of your kraut. Make sure to monitor the temperature and keep it within the safe levels. Ultimately, the ideal temperatures for fermentation are between 68 and 72 degrees Fahrenheit. Fermentation is indicated by the formation of gas bubbles. After fermentation has started (it takes a few days), you can move the crock to a cooler place or lower the temperature. For slow fermentation to take place, the temperature should be around 59 degrees Fahrenheit. During the early stages of fermentation the sauerkraut tends to have an unpleasant odor, so you might want to isolate your project away from living areas, especially during the winter, when windows are closed. Scum will soon form on the surface of the brine. It is important to skim it off every few days after fermentation has started. Wash the cloth and weight and replace on the sauerkraut each time. Note that smaller amounts of cabbage will cure in a shorter time. Twenty pounds of cabbage will cure in 2 to 4 weeks, depending upon the temperature at which it is kept. When properly cured, sauerkraut is yellow-white and free from white spots. Fermentation is complete when bubbling has stopped and no bubbles rise when the crock is tapped.

Storing Sauerkraut in the Refrigerator

Fully fermented kraut may be kept, tightly covered, in the refrigerator for several weeks. That may be a good alternative to the most common storage method (processing in jars) if you make small batches at a time, say 5 to 10 pounds.

Processing Sauerkraut in Jars

For the little amount of time it takes to process your sauerkraut in jars, it's worth canning it, for your sauerkraut can be stored, out of the way, in a clean, dark, and cool place, for a good year and possibly longer.

If you're never canned anything, processing your sauerkraut may be a daunting idea at first. Actually, compared to canning fruits and jams, canning sauerkraut is easy. Not so long ago, before all kinds of fresh fruits and vegetables were available during the winter, people had no choice but to learn how to can vegetables and fruits. The question you may be asking is why should anybody bother to make his or her own sauerkraut when it's available in the store? There are at least two good reasons for making your own sauerkraut. Homemade sauerkraut generally tastes better than store-bought sauerkraut. Many commercial sauerkraut makers pasteurize their product, then add water and more salt to it.

This process destroys some of the good flavor in the raw kraut. Pasteurization also destroys precious enzymes. There is still plenty of goodness to be had, but the kraut's quality is certainly impaired. Okay, the second reason has more to do with Spirit than with anything else. When you make your own sauerkraut, you attach a certain feeling of pride and love for this wonderful vegetable. You can still buy sauerkraut from the store when you're in a pinch, but there is nothing more satisfying than making your own.

The Canning Jars

Jars for canning must be sterilized. Spoilage of sauerkraut will likely occur if this is not done. Wash the jars thoroughly in hot soapy water, then rinse with warm water. Fill a large pot or canning tub with water to about the halfway mark, more or less depending on the size of the jars. Bring to a gentle rolling boil. Place jars, rims down, into the boiling water. At least 95 percent of the entire height of the jar should be submerged in the boiling water. Boil for at least 10 minutes. If you need to replenish the water in the sterilization pot, pour boiling water into the inside of the canner; never pour water directly onto the jars, as that may break them. If making very small batches of sauerkraut, you may be able to let the jars sit in this water until ready to pack with sauerkraut. If you have many jars to sterilize, remove the jars and place on a sterilized surface. Make sure nothing that may contaminate the jars comes into contact with them. Another way to sterilize the jars is to fill them 1/3 full of hot water and placing them in a 275 degree Fahrenheit oven for 30 minutes. A third way to sterilize the jars is to place them in a dishwasher equipped with a sanitation cycle, during which time the temperature is hot enough to successfully sterilize the jars.

Lids and Screwbands

There are various types of jars. They come in standard and wide-mouth openings and have a variety of shapes and sizes. The jars come packed with their closures. The lids are also sold separately, with or without screwbands.

Two-piece Metal Screwbands

With this type of jar, the closure consists of a flat metal disk with its edge flanged to sit accurately on the jar's mouth. The underside of the flange has a rubber-like sealing compound. You must also sterilize the jar closures (lids) and screwbands. During the sealing in hot water, the jars will heat, and as they cool, the snap lid will be sucked down by the vacuum. The lid will be slightly concave. Note: Once the lid has been used it is not reusable, for the sealing compound is misformed and the lid may be bent on opening the jars, thus may not remold properly to another jar. It is not worth the trouble of having your sauerkraut go bad. The lids are not expensive. You may, however, reuse the screwbands, providing they aren't rusted or deteriorated.

Three-piece Glass Lid

This closure consists of a screwband, a flat glass lid, and a separate rubber ring. Soften the rings in hot water for 5 minutes to assure proper molding to the glass. To close, stretch the rubber gently onto the sterilized glass lid. Once the jar is filled with sauerkraut, place the lid on the clean jar rim. Turn the screwband down tight, then given it a ¼ to ½ inch counterturn to allow air in the contents to vent during processing. After finishing processing and removing from the canner, immediately retighten the screwband.

Processing Sauerkraut Using a Water Bath Canner

Pack sauerkraut into the sterilized jars. If there is not enough juice to cover, make a brine by dissolving 2 tablespoons salt in 1 imperial quart of water (5 cups) and add to jars. Leave ½ inch headspace.

Choose a canner that is large enough to process about 4 or 5 quart jars at a time. To keep the jars from getting too hot during processing, which may cause them to crack, you'll need to place some sort of rack on the bottom of the canner. A cake cooling rack or a cluster of 5 or 6 screwbands (ones that are no longer fit to use on jar lids) work fine. Fill the canner with water and heat to a rolling boil. Place the lids and screwbands lightly (not tightly) onto the tops of your jars and place the jars into the canner. Adjust the water in the canner so that the tops are about 1 inch above the water level. Process 15 to 20 minutes for pint jars and 25 to 30 minutes for quart jars in the boiling water bath. After processing is complete, remove the jars from the canner with a jar lifter and place them on a clean cloth or rack. Tighten lids well and let jars stand until completely cooled.

Testing the Seal before Storing Sauerkraut

To make absolutely sure that the jars have properly sealed you may want to test the seal. After the jars have completely cooled off, place the jars upside down on a cloth. After 4 to 8 hours, check the jars for fine opaque foam, which will form in a localized area, indicating a pinpoint leak. Do not confuse this with the large open bubbles inside the jar, which will form when you invert the jar. Store jars in a clean, dark, and cool place. Kraut is best if consumed within a year and it is safe to eat as long as lids remain vacuum-sealed.

Common Causes of Sauerkraut Spoilage

During the fermentation stage, off-flavors and off-odors may develop, which means there is spoilage in the sauerkraut. This is indicated by undesirable colors and soft texture. If any of these problems develop, the sauerkraut should be discarded.

Soft sauerkraut: This may result from:
- Insufficient salt
- Too high temperature during fermentation
- Uneven distribution of salt
- Air pockets caused by improper packing

Pink sauerkraut: The pink color is caused by growth of certain types of yeasts on the surface of the sauerkraut. This may result from:

- Too much salt
- Uneven distribution of salt
- Improper covering or weighing down during fermentation

Rotted sauerkraut: This may be caused by:

- Exposure to air during fermentation

Dark sauerkraut: This may be caused by:

- Unwashed and improperly trimmed cabbage
- Insufficient juice to cover fermenting cabbage
- Uneven distribution of salt
- Exposure to air
- High temperature during fermentation, processing, and storage
- Long storage period.

Freezing Sauerkraut

If you don't have the inclination or time to can your sauerkraut, you can freeze it after it has reached maturity. Freezing it will surely be quicker. Bring kraut and liquid slowly to a boil in a large kettle, stirring frequently. Remove from heat. Cool. Make sure to use good quality food-grade freezer bags, weighing out the sauerkraut in one, two, or three pounds. Unless you are looking to prepare dishes for large groups, it isn't practical to freeze it in quantities larger than that. You may also use pint or quart-size freezer bags, filling them to a level of 3 to 4 inches from their tops. Squeeze as much air as possible from the bag, then seal and label each bag. Before freezing, bags can be inserted into reusable rigid plastic freezer containers for added protection against punctures and leakage. You can also double-bag the sauerkraut or put several small sealed bags of kraut into a larger bag and seal it well. This will prevent the kraut smells to permeate other foods in the freezer. Note: Don't freeze more than 2 pounds of food per cubic foot of freezer capacity per day. Basically, freezing sauerkraut is okay, but some people don't like the results, claiming that the sauerkraut tends to lose some of its crispness, becomes watery, and loses some of its flavor. That alone may be reason enough to process it in jars. Again, do some experimenting. Freeze some sauerkraut and compare it with the canned sauerkraut.

Making Sauerkraut in the Jar

Making sauerkraut in the jar rather than in a crock is a good alternative for people looking to make small batches of sauerkraut at a time. There are various methods of making sauerkraut in the jar. Equal care must be given to the jars, making sure that they are washed and sterilized before filling them with the shredded cabbage. Some people, not wishing to bother with crocks and other containers, prefer to make their sauerkraut exclusively in this way.

Making Sauerkraut in Pint or Quart Jars

Cabbage
2 teaspoons pickling salt for every pound of cut cabbage
Pint or quart canning jars with lids and screwbands

Distribute cut cabbage and salt equally in a food-grade plastic bucket or a large bowl. Mix well. Cover container with a clean towel or food-grade plastic and let sit for 24 hours at room temperature (68 to 72 degrees Fahrenheit) There's a time and temperature tradeoff here. The warmer it is the sooner the kraut will start fermenting. During the 24-hour period, stir the kraut regularly.

Prepare pint or quart jars (wash and rinse thoroughly). Before starting to fill the jars, stir the kraut in the container to ensure it is well mixed. Using a ladle or large spoon, fill the jars, making sure that each jar has equal amounts of kraut and liquid. Pack the kraut down with a wooden spoon or potato masher. Stir the kraut in the container each time you begin filling a new jar to ensure that each jar gets its share of brine. Place a cabbage leaf on top of kraut in each jar. There should be about 1 inch of headspace. After all the jars are filled, top them off with the remaining brine. If there isn't enough brine, add distilled or purified tap water, taking care to distribute it evenly among all the jars. If only chlorinated water is available, note that it must be boiled.

Screw on the lids and set the jars in pans or trays to collect any overflow during the fermentation period. Don't screw the lids on very tightly. They should be just loose enough to allow gas and liquid to escape during fermentation of the kraut. Store at room temperature for 4 to 5 weeks. During this period, invert the jars occasionally to mix the kraut and liquid. After a few turns, set the jars upright back onto the tray.

After about 4 weeks, open a jar and simmer some kraut in a saucepan for 5 minutes, then taste it. If you like it, process the remaining jars. If fermentation is not complete at this stage allow sauerkraut to ferment another week or so, then repeat the taste test. Before processing, rinse the jars, then remove the lids and wipe both the jar top and seal of the lid with a clean wet towel to remove any gunk that would prevent a seal.

Making Sauerkraut in a One-Gallon Jar

Cabbage
4 tablespoons pickling salt for every 6 pounds of cut cabbage [(6 pounds of cabbage for each imperial gallon (5 quarts)]
Imperial gallon jar (wide mouthed)

Note: If using US gallon jars, add 3 ½ tablespoons pickling salt to 5 pounds cut cabbage.

Thoroughly wash, rinse, and dry the jar. Combine the sliced cabbage and pickling salt in a large, food-grade plastic container or a large bowl. Knead the salt into the cabbage and let sit for about 10 minutes, until the cabbage releases its liquid.

Using a wooden spoon or potato masher, pack the cabbage and liquid tightly into the bottom of the glass gallon jar, making sure there are no air pockets. The cabbage will fill about 2/3 of the jar's capacity. Clean the sides of the jar above the level of the cabbage thoroughly. Cabbage should be completely covered by its own juice. If not, add some brine to just cover the cabbage.

Make a brine by adding 1 tablespoon pickling salt to 5 cups water. Bring the brine to a boil, then cool to room temperature. Pour the brine into a durable food-grade 1-gallon plastic bag and seal it well (use a self-sealing bag if possible). Place the brine bag over the cabbage. This will hold it below the surface of the liquid. Even if the bag breaks, the salinity of the kraut will be maintained because of the brine in the bag. Place a brown grocery bag over the jar to shut out any light.

Place the jar in a dark place where it won't be disturbed. Temperature should be between 70 and 75 degrees Fahrenheit, but not any higher, as that may cause the kraut to spoil. Check the jar every two or three days for signs of scum or yeast. If you notice any spoilage, remove it immediately and wash or replace the brine bag and clean the sides of the jar.

The sauerkraut will be ready to eat in 3 to 4 weeks. After fermentation is complete, store sauerkraut, tightly covered, in the refrigerator. Don't store for longer than a few weeks. If sauerkraut spoils, discard it.

Store-bought Sauerkraut

Even if you are not keen on the idea of making your own sauerkraut at home, you can purchase it in most grocery stores. The flavor and quality of commercially made sauerkraut will vary, as not all brands are the same. Sauerkraut comes packed in cans, jars, and plastic bags (in delis). These containers come in various sizes, ranging from small 16-ounce cans or jars to 2 ½-quart containers, and even larger.

To Rinse or Not to Rinse Sauerkraut

The sodium content in the brine of commercially made sauerkraut varies a lot. With some brands I tried, the sodium content was very high, making it necessary to rinse the sauerkraut with cold water before using. Most of the recipes in this book indicate whether or not to rinse the sauerkraut, be it homemade or store-bought, but this preference is generally left to the individual. How thoroughly you rinse the kraut is up to you. Some people prefer not to rinse their sauerkraut at all. In most cases, it depends somewhat on the recipe itself. Consider that rather than rinsing the sauerkraut, you may reduce the amount of salt the recipe suggests or eliminate it entirely. I have tried to maintain a healthy balance throughout in the area of salt with the recipes presented here. However, people on sodium-reduced diets should rinse their kraut very thoroughly. Many people are misinformed about the salt factor when eating kraut. The truth is that sauerkraut, especially when rinsed, doesn't have more salt than many canned soups. A cup of rinsed sauerkraut (more or less depending on how well you rinse it) has only about 840 milligrams of sodium, while a cup of Campbell's chicken noodle soup has 980. For most people one serving of sauerkraut is about ½ to 1cup. So if you must reduce your sodium intake, but still enjoy the benefits of sauerkraut in your diet, rinse the kraut with cold water before using.

How Much Sauerkraut to Add

While preparing the recipes in this book I looked at thousands of sauerkraut recipes in books and on the World Wide Web, many of which were virtually the same, yet the amount of sauerkraut in almost identical recipes often varied. I think this is because people have different preferences as to how much sauerkraut constitutes a serving. I've tried to stay as close to the original recipes without altering them too much. Still, my own ideas influenced my decisions more often than not. Either way, unless the recipe is very small, the amount of sauerkraut varying by 1 cup will not make a big difference. With certain recipes, particularly baked items, it is important to use precise amounts. Soups and stews give you more flexibility. Also note that in most recipes, I indicate the amounts in cups, ounces, or pounds. The reason for that is because of the differences between the imperial quart and the US quart. Whenever I give measurements of ingredients in quarts, I am using the imperial quart as a guide, which equals 5 cups, as opposed to the US quart, which equals 4 cups.

Sauerkraut Breads

Sauerkraut Rye Bread
(For Bread Machine)

¾ cup plus 1 tablespoon water
2 tablespoons molasses
2 tablespoons soft butter
1 cup sauerkraut, drained and chopped
1 tablespoon caraway seed
2 tablespoons brown sugar
1 ½ teaspoons salt
1 cup rye flour
2 cups all-purpose flour
2 ¼ teaspoons active dry yeast

- Follow instructions given by the manufacturer of your bread machine as bread machines vary somewhat. It is important to place all ingredients in the order suggested by the manufacturer, which may not be how they are listed here. It is equally important to measure out the ingredients precisely. For this recipe, select the basic bread setting and turn the time feature setting off.
- Check dough after 5 minutes of mixing. It is important to listen to your machine while it's kneading and adjust the wet and dry ratio if needed. The dough should be forming into a smooth satiny ball. If the dough looks dry and cracked, add 1 to 2 tablespoons water. If it looks flat and wet, add 1 to 2 tablespoons flour.
- This recipe will make 1 2-pound loaf of bread.

Sauerkraut Rye Bread

2 ½ - 2 ¾ cups white all-purpose flour
2 cups dark rye flour
2 packages instant dry yeast
½ cup instant skim milk powder
2 tablespoons sugar
1 tablespoon caraway seeds
½ tablespoon salt
½ tablespoon ginger
1 ½ cups water
¼ cup oil
1 cup sauerkraut, with a bit of juice

- In a large mixing bowl, combine 1 cup white flour with ½ cup rye flour, yeast, skim milk powder, sugar, caraway seeds, salt, and ginger; mix well.
- In a small skillet or saucepan, heat water and oil until quite warm, but not hot. Add to flour mixture and stir with a whisk until dry ingredients are moistened. Stir in sauerkraut and mix well. Slowly, while stirring then kneading, add remaining rye flour and all-purpose flour to make a firm dough. (The amount of flour will depend on how much juice the sauerkraut has). Knead on a lightly floured surface for about 5 minutes, until dough is smooth and elastic.
- Divide dough into two equal parts. Shape each part into an oblong shape. Place in greased 8x4-inch loaf pans. Brush dough lightly with oil. Cover and let dough rise in warm place until light and doubled, about 1 hour.
- Bake at 375 degrees Fahrenheit for 45 to 50 minutes until loaves sound hollow when tapped. If loaves get too dark, cover with foil for the last 15 minutes of baking. Remove from pans and place on a rack to cool.
- Makes 2 loaves.

Cottage Cheese Kraut Bread

1 tablespoon active dry yeast
2 tablespoons light brown sugar
½ cup warm water
½ cup cottage cheese
2 tablespoons butter or shortening
1 teaspoon salt
1 teaspoon caraway or dill seeds
1 tablespoon minced onion
1 egg, beaten
2 ¼ cups flour
1 cup sauerkraut, rinsed, drained, and chopped

- Combine yeast, sugar, and ½ cup water. Stir to mix; let stand for about 5 to 7 minutes, until foaming.
- Put cottage cheese, butter, caraway seeds, and salt into a saucepan; heat to slightly warmer than lukewarm. Transfer to a mixing bowl and stir in yeast mixture and beaten egg. Add sauerkraut and mix thoroughly. The temperature of mixture should be lukewarm.
- Add 1 ¼ cups flour while beating mixture with a wooden spoon. Add remaining flour and knead mixture into a dough.
- Turn dough out onto a floured surface and knead for 3 to 5 minutes. Put dough into a greased bowl, cover with a cloth, and set in a warm place until double in size, about 1 ½ hours. Punch dough down and shape it into a loaf. Put dough into a greased 8x4x3-inch bread loaf pan. Let rise again until double in size.
- Preheat oven to 375 degrees Fahrenheit. Bake bread for 35 to 40 minutes. Bread is done when crust makes a hollow sound when tapped.
- Makes 1 loaf.

Sauerkraut Beer Bread

1 cup sauerkraut, rinsed, drained, and chopped
1 ½ cups dark rye flour
3 cups unbleached white flour
¼ cup light brown sugar
1 tablespoon baking powder
¾ teaspoon salt
1 teaspoon caraway seeds
5 tablespoons cooking oil
1 2/3 cups beer

- Preheat the oven to 350 degrees Fahrenheit.
- In a large mixing bowl, combine the flours, sugar, baking powder, salt, and caraway seeds; mix well. Form a well in the center and, while stirring, slowly add the oil and beer to form a sticky dough. Add the sauerkraut and mix well.
- Transfer dough to a well-greased 9x5x3-inch bread loaf pan.
- Bake in preheated oven for 50 to 60 minutes.
- This bread is best served warm.
- Makes one loaf.

Sauerkraut Onion Bread

1 ½ tablespoons white sugar
1 tablespoon active dry yeast
½ cup water
1 cup hot milk
2 tablespoons cooking oil
½ tablespoon caraway seeds
1 teaspoon salt
¼ teaspoon onion salt
½ cup sauerkraut, drained, rinsed, and finely chopped
1 tablespoon finely chopped onion
1 cup rye flour
1 cup whole wheat flour
1 ¾ - 2 cups all-purpose flour

- In a small bowl, combine sugar, yeast, and water; stir to mix. Let stand for 5 to 7 minutes, until foaming.
- In a large mixing bowl, combine yeast mixture, milk, oil, caraway seeds, and salts; stir to mix. Mix in sauerkraut and onion. While beating, then kneading, add rye flour and whole-wheat flour. Add 1 ¾ cups all-purpose flour while continue kneading. Turn out onto a floured board and knead for about 10 minutes, adding remaining flour as needed. Knead into a semi-smooth dough.
- Place dough in a large greased bowl and set in a warm place; let rise for about an hour, until double in size. Punch down and place in a greased 9x6x4-inch bread loaf pan; let rise until double in size, 30 to 40 minutes.
- Preheat oven to 350 degrees Fahrenheit. Put pan in oven and bake for 45 to 50 minutes. Brush top with butter after baking bread for about 10 minutes.
- Makes 1 loaf.

Sauerkraut Gingerbread

½ cup shortening
1 cup brown sugar
2 medium eggs
2 teaspoons orange rind, grated
2 cups white flour
1 teaspoon nutmeg
1 teaspoon baking soda
½ teaspoon salt
1 ½ teaspoons ginger
½ cup boiling water
½ cup molasses
1 cup sauerkraut

- Put all ingredients except sauerkraut into a mixing bowl and blend well with electric mixer for about 2 minutes.
- Rinse sauerkraut with cold water, drain, and chop it coarsely. Blend into batter.
- Grease an 8x11-inch baking pan and add batter. Bake at 350 degrees Fahrenheit for 40 minutes.
- Serve hot with applesauce or whipped cream.

Krauted Appetizers

Krauted Cheese # 1

1 4-ounce package cream cheese, softened
2 tablespoons mayonnaise
1/3 cup blue cheese
1 teaspoon lemon juice
2 tablespoons finely chopped green pepper
2 tablespoons minced celery
¼ cup chopped walnuts
1 ¾ cups sauerkraut, rinsed, drained, and chopped
Finely chopped walnuts

- Soften cream cheese and blend with mayonnaise, blue cheese, and lemon juice until smooth. Mix in green pepper, celery, ¼ cup walnuts, and sauerkraut.
- Chill briefly in refrigerator. Form into one large ball or 2 smaller balls and roll in finely chopped walnuts. Refrigerate.
- Serve on platter surrounded with crackers.

Krauted Cheese # 2

1 cup sauerkraut, with some juice
8 ounces cheddar cheese, finely grated
16 ounces Swiss cheese, finely grated
1 clove garlic, minced
1 teaspoon powdered mustard
2 teaspoons Worcestershire sauce
½ teaspoons pepper

- Finely chop sauerkraut. Mix with all other ingredients and, using your hands, work to a smooth texture. Add more sauerkraut juice if necessary for a smooth blend. Cover and refrigerate. Serve at room temperature.

Kraut Knishes
(Jewish)

Dough
3 cups flour
½ teaspoon baking powder
¼ teaspoon salt
Dash pepper
4 ounces butter
2 eggs, beaten (save some for glaze)
1 ½ cups mashed potatoes

Filling # 1
1 ½ cups ground meat (browned) or 1 ½ cups cooked buckwheat (not too mushy)
1 cup sauerkraut, rinsed, drained, and chopped
1 medium onion, minced (1 cup)
2 cloves garlic, minced
½ teaspoon caraway seeds
½ teaspoon salt
1/8 teaspoon pepper

Filling # 2
2 tablespoons butter, for sautéing
1 cup chopped onions
2 cups sauerkraut, rinsed, drained, chopped, then sautéed with onions for 10 minutes
1 teaspoon caraway seeds
1 tablespoon brown sugar

- In a mixing bowl, combine baking powder, salt, and pepper. Mix well. Cut butter into flour. Using hands, crumble till well mixed. Add about two thirds of the beaten eggs; add all of the mashed potatoes. Mix and work into a soft dough. Knead until smooth. Many knish recipes suggest chilling the dough, but on occasion, pressed for time, I've tried it while dough was still warm, and still had good results.
- Combine the filling ingredients of your choice and mix well.
- Divide the dough in four parts. On a lightly floured surface, roll out one part 7x11 inches and 1/8 inch thick. Place 2/3 to ¾ cup filling on top and spread out evenly. Roll the dough and filling up tightly like a jellyroll. Cut into 1-inch pieces. Place cut side down on a well greased baking sheet. Repeat with the remaining dough.
- Bake knishes in the oven at 375 degrees Fahrenheit for 30 minutes. After baking for 15 minutes, brush knishes with beaten egg and bake until golden brown.
- Makes 24 knishes.

Kraut Appetizers

1 small onion, finely chopped
1 ½ tablespoons butter
½ cup finely chopped cooked ham
½ cup finely chopped corned beef
1 clove garlic, crushed
3 tablespoons flour
1 medium egg, beaten
1 cup sauerkraut, rinsed and thoroughly drained (chopped)
1/8 teaspoon seasoning salt
1/8 teaspoon Worcestershire sauce
½ tablespoon chopped parsley
1 ¼ cups milk
1 ¼ cups sifted all-purpose flour
1 cup fine dry breadcrumbs
Vegetable oil

- Cook chopped onion in butter over low heat for 5 minutes. Stir in ham, corned beef, and garlic. Cook for 10 minutes, stirring occasionally. Blend in the flour and the egg. Stir in the sauerkraut, seasonings, and ¼ cup milk. Cook over low heat, stirring occasionally, until thickened. Put in refrigerator to chill through.
- Shape mixture into approximately 28 balls the size of walnuts. Combine 1 cup milk and 1 ¼ cups flour; stir to mix. Coat balls in mixture; roll in breadcrumbs. Fry in deep vegetable oil for 2 to 3 minutes or until light brown. Place on paper towels to absorb excess oil. Insert a toothpick in each of the balls.
- You may freeze appetizers if not serving immediately. Shape sauerkraut mixture into balls; place in freezer container, dividing layers with foil or freezer wrap. Freeze, making sure the container is well sealed. Before serving, remove from freezer and partially thaw at room temperature 1 hour before serving time. Increase frying time by about 1 minute. Insert toothpicks and serve. Makes 28 appetizers.

Chicken Liver and Bacon Appetizers with Sweet and Sour Sauce

Appetizers
1 pound chicken livers, divided in 20 pieces
10 strips thinly sliced bacon, cut in half crosswise
Freshly ground pepper
1 teaspoon caraway seeds, crushed
Sweet and Sour Sauce
½ cup plus 1 tablespoon sauerkraut juice
1 tablespoon corn starch
2 tablespoons honey

Optional: For extra sauerkraut flavor, marinate livers in 1 cup sauerkraut juice for 1 hour before assembling appetizers.

- Wrap each chicken liver piece with a bacon strip; place in a jellyroll pan or rectangular casserole. Sprinkle with pepper and caraway seeds. Broil under high heat in the oven for 15 minutes, until chicken livers are cooked through.
- Pour ½ cup sauerkraut juice into a small skillet or saucepan. Heat over low heat. Combine 1 tablespoon sauerkraut juice and cornstarch; stir to dissolve cornstarch. Add honey and cornstarch mixture to pan and heat, stirring, until honey is melted and mixture has thickened to the consistency of a thin syrup.
- Use sauce as a dip for the appetizers or drip sauce over top.
- Insert a toothpick in each appetizer. Excellent eaten warm or cold.
- Makes 20 appetizers.

Sauerkraut Balls

4 cups sauerkraut, drained, squeezed, and finely chopped
3 tablespoons butter
1 medium onion, finely chopped
1 clove garlic, crushed
1 cup cooked ham, diced
1 cup cooked corned beef, diced
6 tablespoons flour
3 eggs
1/8 teaspoon seasoning salt
½ teaspoon Worcestershire sauce
1 tablespoon fresh parsley, chopped
½ cup beef stock or bouillon
2 tablespoons water
Fine cracker meal

- Melt butter in large skillet. Add onion and garlic, and cook over low heat for 5 to 7 minutes. Add ham and corned beef. While stirring, sprinkle in flour and cook until brown.
- Add 1 egg, sauerkraut, seasoning salt, Worcestershire sauce, parsley, and beef stock. Cook over low heat, stirring occasionally, until thickened. Remove from heat and chill.
- Shape chilled mixture into walnut-sized balls.
- Beat remaining eggs with water; dip balls in egg mixture, and then roll in cracker meal. Deep fry at 375 degrees Fahrenheit for 2 to 3 minutes, or until brown. Place on non-bleached napkin to drain off excess fat. Serve warm.
- You may freeze sauerkraut balls. After rolling in cracker meal, place balls on a cookie sheet, freeze, and then put them into plastic freezer bags. Thaw before deep-frying.
- Recipe makes 25 to 30 balls.

Kraut Balls with Mustard Dip

1 tablespoon vegetable oil
1 medium onion, minced
2 clove garlic, minced
8 ounces cooked ham, chopped
4 cups sauerkraut rinsed, dried, and chopped
1 teaspoon dry mustard
½ - ¾ cup fine bread crumbs
Pepper to taste
2 tablespoons fresh parsley, minced
1 egg white, frothed
½ cup flour
1 egg, lightly beaten
1 cup breadcrumbs
Vegetable oil or shortening, for frying
2/3 cup light mayonnaise
4 teaspoons prepared yellow mustard

- In a small skillet, heat vegetable oil over medium high heat; sauté onion and garlic for about 3 minutes, stirring frequently, until onion is soft.
- In a large mixing bowl, combine onion with ham, sauerkraut, dry mustard, ½ cup breadcrumbs, pepper, parsley, and egg white; mix well. Add more breadcrumbs if mixture is too wet. Using hands, form 1 ½-inch balls.
- Pour vegetable oil (or melt shortening), in a heavy saucepan to a depth of 2 inches. Heat to 375 degrees Fahrenheit.
- While oil is heating, put ½ cup flour, 1 beaten egg, and 1 cup bread crumbs in separate shallow bowls and set next to each other, within easy reach. Coat sauerkraut balls in flour, then egg and finally the breadcrumbs. Fry sauerkraut balls in batches until they are browned and crisp, about 3 minutes, turning to ensure even browning.
- In a small bowl combine mayonnaise and prepared yellow mustard; mix until smooth. Serve alongside kraut balls as a dip. Serves 12.

Quick Kraut Balls

8 ounces cream cheese, softened
¾ cup sauerkraut, drained and finely chopped
1/3 cup diced cooked smoked sausage
2 tablespoons minced onion
4 teaspoons Worcestershire sauce.
½ cup toasted rye bread crumbs

- Combine cream cheese, sauerkraut, sausage, onion, and Worcestershire sauce. Form small walnut-sized balls and roll them in the breadcrumbs.
- Refrigerate for at least an hour before serving.
- Yields about 3 dozen balls.

Spicy Kraut and Sausage Balls

1 pound uncooked spicy bratwurst or similar pork sausages
1 onion, diced
2 cups sauerkraut, rinsed, drained, and chopped
2 teaspoons brown Dijon prepared mustard
1 tablespoon parsley
2 teaspoons crushed caraway seeds (optional)
1 8-ounce package cream cheese, softened
1 teaspoon garlic salt
2 quarts vegetable oil, for frying
1 ½ cups flour
1 ¼ cups milk
1 egg, lightly beaten
2 cups seasoned fine bread crumbs

- Peel the skins off the sausages and mash the sausage meat in a large skillet; blend in diced onion. Cook over medium-high heat for about 10 minutes, until sausage meat is evenly browned and onions are soft. Drain and transfer to a large bowl.

46

- Thoroughly mix sauerkraut, mustard, parsley, crushed caraway seeds, cream cheese, and garlic salt with the sausage mixture. Cover and chill in the refrigerator for 2 hours.
- Heat oil in deep fryer or large heavy saucepan to 375 degrees Fahrenheit.
- Arrange three bowls within easy reach, putting the flour in a one bowl, milk and eggs (blended) in the second, and seasoned bread crumbs in the third.
- Roll the chilled sausage mixture into 1-inch balls. As you roll balls, dredge each in the flour, then the egg and milk mixture, then finally the bread crumbs. In small batches, deep-fry the sausage balls in the preheated oil for about 3 minutes, until golden brown. Remove with a slotted spoon and place on paper towels to drain. Insert a toothpick in each ball and arrange balls on a serving platter. Serve warm.
- Makes 30 to 35 balls.

Reuben Rolls

1 12-ounce can corned beef, flaked
2 cups sauerkraut, rinsed and drained
4 ounces Swiss cheese, shredded
½ cup Russian salad dressing
18 - 20 sheets of 11x17-inch Phyllo pastry (flaky pastry dough)
Butter

- In a bowl, corned beef, sauerkraut, Swiss cheese, and Russian salad dressing.
- Follow instruction in box on thawing out the dough. Because it dries out fast, you will need to work quickly or lay a damp towel over the exposed pastry once you take it out of the box. You can make pockets, rolls, or triangles. Rolls are the easiest to make.
- Place two sheets of pastry on a flat surface, with the narrow side facing you. Place some filling along the edge, then roll up the pastry. Cut the roll into 4 to 5 small rolls and place them into a lightly greased square casserole dish or a roasting pan. For this recipe you'll need two 9x13-inch pans, or bake the rolls in 2 batches.
- Brush rolls liberally with melted butter. Place into a preheated 350 degree Fahrenheit oven and bake about 15 minutes, until rolls are golden brown.
- Serve with sour cream, plum sauce, or a creamy dip of your choice.
- Yields about 48 rolls, more or less depending on size of rolls.

Kraut Strudel

1 1/3 cups finely chopped onions
5 tablespoons melted butter
1 cup chopped cooked ham or corned beef (not from a can)
1 ½ cups sauerkraut
1 10-ounce can condensed beef consommé
1 teaspoon caraway seeds
2 teaspoons brown sugar
2 teaspoons flour
4 to 8 sheets 11x17-inch Phyllo pastry (flaky pastry dough)

- Preheat oven to 375 degrees Fahrenheit.
- Using a large skillet, cook onions in 3 tablespoons butter for about 5 minutes over low heat. Add cooked ham, sauerkraut, beef consommé, caraway seeds, and brown sugar; stir to mix. Cook for another 5 minutes to blend, then stir in flour and heat until thickened.
- Follow instructions on Phyllo pastry package. Assemble strudel using 1 sheet, or double by using 2 sheets, depending on your preference in the thickness of the pastry. Place sheets on a lightly greased flat surface and place ¼ of the filling mixture evenly at the narrow end. Roll up like a jelly roll and cut each roll in four equal pieces crosswise. Place rolls, seam side down, on a lightly greased jelly roll pan. Assemble remaining strudel. Brush tops and sides of rolls with remaining butter. Instead of butter for brushing rolls, you may use an egg wash (1 beaten egg). **Note:** It is important to work fast once you've removed the pastry sheets from the package, as they dry very fast. The instructions on the box suggest using up all the pastry once it is unthawed, but I've found that it is okay to refreeze it. The main concern is to not let it sit in the open air, allowing it to dry out. To keep the pastry waiting to be rolled moist, lay a moist cloth over top.
- Place pan in the oven and bake strudel for about 10 minutes, until golden brown.
- Makes 16 strudel appetizers.

Sauerkraut Soups, Borschts, and Stews

Kraut Fruit Soup

2 cups sauerkraut
4 oranges
1 ½ cups watermelon chunks
1 cup crushed pineapple
1 cup red grapes
1 cup green grapes
1 sweet apple, cored and chopped

- Rinse and drain sauerkraut.
- Peel oranges and cut each into small pieces. Crush grapes, reserving the juice.
- In a serving bowl, combine all the fruit, sauerkraut, and juices; mix well. Cover bowl with plastic wrap and chill before serving.
- Serves 4.

Russian Sauerkraut Soup

2 tablespoons dried white mushrooms
2 onions, chopped
1 leek (white part only)
1 large carrot, chopped
2 ounces celery root, chopped
1 large parsley root, chopped
1 teaspoon salt
1 ½ pounds sauerkraut, rinsed and drained
½ cup fresh mushrooms
2 medium potatoes
1 celery stalk, chopped
2 tablespoons butter
¼ teaspoon black pepper
2 bay leaves
1 teaspoon marjoram
2 teaspoons parsley
2 teaspoons dill weed
5 cloves garlic, minced
½ cup sour cream mixed with 3 tablespoons cream

- Soak dried mushrooms in cold water to cover for 3 hours or boil in water for 20 minutes. Drain and set aside.
- To make a vegetable stock, put half of the onions, leek, carrot, celery root, and parsley root in a 4-quart pot. Set the rest of the vegetables aside. Add 10 cups water to the pot. Add salt. Bring to a boil, then reduce heat to low and simmer, partially covered, for 45 to 60 minutes. Strain stock, discarding the vegetables.
- Wash the drained soaked mushrooms and the fresh mushrooms. Put both into a small pot, add water to cover, and cook over low heat for about 20 minutes. Drain; chop mushrooms.
- Peel the potatoes and cut into ½ to ¾-inch cubes.
- Dice the remaining vegetables, including the celery; sauté gently in the butter, stirring often, until soft, about 10 minutes.

- Combine vegetable stock, sauerkraut, mushrooms, potatoes, sautéed vegetables, pepper, bay leaves, marjoram, parsley, and dill weed. Simmer, uncovered, for 15 minutes or until potatoes are cooked. Add the garlic, cover the pot, turn off the heat, and let stand for 10 minutes. Remove the bay leaves before serving.
- Pour the soup into a heated tureen, add the sour cream dressing, and serve in heated soup bowls.
- Serves 6.

Sauerkraut Bulgur Soup
(Armenian)

½ cup onion, chopped
¼ cup butter
3 cups sauerkraut
1/3 cup tomato puree
1 large potato, diced
½ cup fine bulgur wheat
8 to 10 cups chicken stock
Salt and pepper to taste
1 green pepper, finely sliced
Fresh parsley, for garnish

- In a soup pot, sauté onion over medium heat in butter until golden.
- Rinse, drain, and chop sauerkraut. Add to pot and cook until soft, adding water if mixture gets too dry. Add tomato puree and cook for 5 to 7 minutes. Add potatoes, bulgur wheat, and stock; cook for about 15 minutes. Season to taste with salt and pepper. Garnish with green pepper and parsley.
- Serves 4.

Sauerkraut Soup in the Crockpot

4 cups sauerkraut
2 pounds short ribs
½ cup brown sugar
2 cloves garlic, crushed
1 19-ounce canned tomatoes
Water
5 gingersnaps, crushed (optional)

- Put all the ingredients except gingersnaps in the crockpot; add water to cover about 1 inch. Cover tightly and cook on low temperature 10 to 12 hours, stirring occasionally, until meat is fork tender.
- Thirty minutes before serving, remove the short ribs from soup and let cool slightly. Skim off fat. Remove meat from bones and cut in bite-size pieces, removing as much fat and gristle as you can. Return meat to soup, along with the crushed gingersnaps. Cook another 30 minutes before serving.

Potato Sauerkraut Soup in the Crockpot

4 cups chicken broth
1 10-ounce can cream of mushroom soup
3 cups sauerkraut, rinsed and drained
8 ounces mushrooms, sliced
3 medium potatoes, cubed
2 medium carrots, chopped
1 medium onion, chopped
2 cloves garlic, chopped
2 stalks celery, chopped
1 pound smoked Polish sausages, or similar
2 tablespoons apple-cider vinegar
2 teaspoons dill weed
½ teaspoon pepper
2 slices bacon

- Put all ingredients except bacon into a large crockpot; stir to mix well. Cover and cook on low heat for 8 to 10 hours, or until vegetables are tender.
- A few minutes before soup is done, fry bacon to crisp; drain and crumble. Skim fat off soup. Sprinkle each serving with bacon bits.
- Serves 6.

Sauerkraut Soup

2 cups sauerkraut
1 medium-large potato (½ pound)
3 - 4 cups beef stock
½ teaspoon caraway seeds
1 ½ tablespoons flour
1 egg
1 cup light cream
Salt and pepper to taste
A bit of lemon juice, if desired
Paprika

- Rinse, drain, and chop the sauerkraut. Peel and dice the potato. Put vegetables into a saucepan and add stock. Add caraway seeds. Cook until potatoes are tender.
- Blend the flour in a little water and add to saucepan to thicken soup. Boil for a minute or two. Beat the egg and cream together; stir into the soup. Bring to a boil. Season to taste with salt and pepper; add lemon juice, if desired. Serve with a sprinkle of paprika in each bowl.
- Serves 4.

Lithuanian Sparerib Sauerkraut Soup

2 ½ - 3 pounds spareribs
3 quarts water
2 medium onions, sliced
2 cloves chopped garlic (optional)
2 - 3 bay leaves
2 teaspoons salt
6 to 8 peppercorns
4 cups sauerkraut, rinsed
1 small head of cabbage, shredded

- Put ribs into a pot; add water, onion, garlic, bay leaves, and peppercorns. Bring to a boil, then reduce heat to medium-low and cook about 1 hour.
- Add sauerkraut and cook 30 minutes. Add cabbage and boil another 45 minutes, adding more water if necessary (depending on the size of cabbage). Ribs may be removed from pot and served separately, or the meat cut into pieces and placed in the soup. Serve with rye bread or hot boiled potatoes.
- Serves 6.

Peasant Soup

2 pounds beef roast (with some bone)
2 tablespoons cooking oil
1 medium onion, chopped
1 pound carrots, sliced
3 stalks celery, chopped
1 tablespoon salt
1 teaspoon black pepper
1 teaspoon dill seeds
¼ cup chopped parsley
2 pounds cabbage, shredded
4 cups sauerkraut, with juice
3 cloves garlic, minced
1 tablespoons butter
5 medium tomatoes, peeled and quartered

- Heat 2 tablespoons oil in a large heavy pot and brown meat on all sides. Add onions, carrots, celery, salt, pepper, dill seeds, parsley, and water (14 cups). Cover and cook over low heat for 1 ½ to 2 hours, until meat is tender. Remove meat from pot and set aside.
- In a large skillet, melt butter. Add the cabbage, sauerkraut, and garlic; sauté until cabbage wilts. Add to pot, along with tomatoes, and simmer, covered, for another hour. Cut meat into bite sized pieces, return to pot and heat through.
- Serves 12.

Polish-Style Chicken and Kielbasa Soup

4 tablespoons butter
1 pound, boneless, skinless chicken, cut into bite-size pieces
1 cup chopped onions
2 cloves garlic, minced
1 tart apple, cored and chopped
2 cups sauerkraut, rinsed and drained
2 14-ounce cans stewed tomatoes
1 teaspoon prepared mustard
2 ½ cups chicken stock
Or:
1 10-ounce can condensed chicken broth mixed with 10 ounces water
6 small new potatoes, cubed
1 link Kielbasa, cut in ¾-inch slices
¾ teaspoon caraway seeds
Salt and black pepper to taste

- Melt 2 tablespoons butter in a large pot over medium heat; add chicken and cook, stirring, until lightly browned. Reduce heat to medium-low, add the remaining butter, along with the onions, garlic, and apple. Cook until the onion is tender.
- Stir in the sauerkraut, stewed tomatoes (with juice), mustard, and half of stock. Add potatoes, sausage, and caraway seeds. Place lid on pot and simmer for 1 to 1 ¼ hours, or until vegetables are tender.
- Add the remaining stock, bring to a boil, then shut off heat. Season with salt and pepper to taste. Serve with whole-wheat or rye bread.
- Serves 6.

Polish Kraut Soup

2 pounds smoked pork shanks
5 - 6 cups water
1 medium-large onion, chopped
4 cups sauerkraut juice
¼ cup sugar
1 egg
¼ cup light cream
¾ cup milk
1 tablespoon flour or cornstarch

- Put meat and water into a pot and cook until meat is well done. Add onion, sauerkraut juice, and sugar. Beat egg; mix with cream and milk and stir in flour or cornstarch. Add to soup and bring to a boil. Serve with potatoes or potato dumplings.
- Serves 5 to 6.

Sauerkraut Soup

4 cups sauerkraut
6 or more cups beef stock
4 slices bacon, chopped
2 large onions, chopped
1 teaspoon paprika
2 tablespoons tomato paste
½ teaspoon caraway seeds
Salt and pepper
2 potatoes, peeled, grated, and soaked in water
¼ pound cooked ham or corned beef, diced
2 beef wieners, sliced

- In a large saucepan or small pot, cook sauerkraut over low heat with 3 cups beef stock for about 30 minutes.
- In a skillet, fry bacon. When some fat has been rendered, add onions and sauté until golden. Add paprika, remaining stock, tomato paste, caraway seeds, and salt and pepper to taste. Stir to mix; cook for 2 minutes.
- Add ingredients in skillet to sauerkraut. Drain potatoes and add to soup. Simmer 20 to 30 minutes, adding more beef stock (or water) if necessary. Add ham or corned beef and wieners. Cook until meats are heated through.
- Serves 6.

Rich Sauerkraut Soup

1 10-ounce can cream of mushroom and garlic soup
1 10-ounce can cream of chicken soup
2 ½ cups water
4 cups homemade chicken broth
OR
1 10-ounce can condensed chicken broth and 2 ¾ cups water
1 medium onion, finely chopped
1 ¾ cups sliced carrots
1 ¾ cups sliced potatoes
2 - 3 cups sauerkraut, with a bit of juice
1 pound smoked uncooked sausage, sliced or coarsely chopped
2 teaspoons dried dill weed
Salt and pepper

- In a large pot, combine mushroom and garlic soup, chicken soup, and 2 ½ cups water. Bring to a boil over medium-high heat. Stir in chicken broth, carrots, potatoes, and onion. Simmer for 10 minutes. Add sauerkraut, sausages, and dill weed. Simmer for 45 to 60 minutes, until soup has thickened slightly. Taste soup and season with salt and pepper to taste.
- Serves 6.

Beet and Sauerkraut Soup

2 medium onions, chopped
4 cloves garlic, chopped
2 tablespoons olive oil
3 cups sauerkraut, with a bit of juice
3 large beets, peeled and chopped, (plus a few leaves, if available)
Vegetable broth
¼ teaspoon each of salt and pepper
1 7 ½-ounce can tomato sauce (optional)
Fresh parsley and basil, chopped

- Sauté onions and garlic in oil until soft. Put into a pot; add sauerkraut and beets, then pour in broth to cover. Season with salt and pepper.
- Cook over low heat for 1 to 1 ½ hours, until beets are tender. Ten minutes before soup is done, stir in tomato sauce, if desired, and add parsley and basil. Taste soup and add more salt if preferred.
- Serve with whole wheat bread or rye bread. For a unique flavor, instead of butter, spread bread with a very thin layer of vegemite. Vegemite is a concentrated yeast spread that adds a tangy flavor to breads and sandwiches.
- Serves 5 to 6.

Sauerkraut Buckwheat Soup

2 pounds chicken or turkey pieces (with some fat)
12 cups water
1 cup buckwheat
1 ½ cups sauerkraut
¼ - ½ cup sauerkraut juice
2 teaspoons salt
¼ teaspoon black pepper
2 eggs, lightly beaten

- Place chicken or turkey pieces into a pot. Add water to cover or slightly more, about 12 cups. Bring to a boil, then reduce heat and cook over low heat for an hour, until meat is tender. Remove meat and strain broth; set meat aside.
- While meat is cooking, rinse buckwheat with hot water and let soak in water for about 20 minutes.
- Add buckwheat to stock and cook over low heat for 10 minutes. Add sauerkraut, sauerkraut juice, salt, and pepper, and cook another 10 to 15 minutes. Two minutes before serving, stir in eggs and cook just until eggs are cooked.
- Serve soup alongside meat. Serves 6.

Sauerkraut Soup with Fish Heads
(Russian)

2 ½ pounds salmon, sturgeon or trout heads
Cold water
3 medium onions
Salt and pepper to taste
4 - 5 cups sauerkraut, lightly rinsed and drained
¼ cup oil or butter
1 tablespoon flour
Water
1 bunch parsley

- Rinse fish heads and put into a large pot. Add cold water to cover and bring to a boil. Reduce heat and simmer for about 45 minutes. Skim broth and add 1 onion (quartered), and salt and pepper, then continue simmering until meat falls off the bones.
- Strain broth; reserve fish in a covered dish.
- Using a skillet, sauté sauerkraut and remaining onions (chopped) in oil or butter. Add to broth and simmer for 30 minutes until sauerkraut is tender. Dissolve flour in a bit of water and add to soup to thicken.
- Transfer fish to a soup tureen; pour hot soup over it and garnish with parsley.
- Serves 4.

Meatless Sauerkraut Soup

4 cups sauerkraut
½ pound sliced fresh mushrooms
3 quarts water
2 tablespoons shortening
1 onion, chopped
1 cup cooked potatoes, diced
2 tablespoons flour
3 tablespoons butter
1 teaspoon salt, to taste
¼ teaspoon black pepper, to taste

- Rinse and drain sauerkraut. Put sauerkraut and mushrooms into a pot; add water. Bring to a boil, then reduce heat and simmer for about 30 minutes.
- Meanwhile, sauté onion in shortening. Add to soup.
- Using a small skillet or saucepan, brown flour in butter over medium heat. Add to soup along with diced potatoes and seasonings. Continue simmering for another 20 to 25 minutes, then serve.

Lentil Sauerkraut Soup

1 ¼ cups dried lentils
4 cups water
½ cup butter or margarine
½ cup white flour or cornstarch
1 cup sauerkraut
Salt and black pepper
1 cup sour cream

- Wash and drain the lentils, cover with water and soak for 2 hours. Keep adding more water to cover as lentils soak up liquid.

- Bring lentils to a quick boil, then reduce heat; cover and simmer over medium heat until the lentils are tender.
- Thicken soup with butter and flour mixture. Add Sauerkraut and continue cooking for about 20 minutes. Season to taste with salt and pepper.
- Arrange soup in bowls; add a dollop of sour cream to each bowl.
- Serves 6 to 8.

Day After Thanksgiving Soup

Never throw out the bones of your Thanksgiving turkey. Soup the next day ought to be as much a tradition as the Thanksgiving meal itself. Here's a zesty and nutritious soup you can make from leftovers.

4 imperial quarts (20 cups) turkey stock
10 medium-sized fresh or frozen tomatoes, cut
About 5 cups leftover boiled potatoes, chopped or mashed
1 cup corn or peas (optional)
One large onion, chopped
4 cloves garlic, finely chopped
5 cups sauerkraut, lightly rinsed
Salt and black pepper to taste

- Make stock from turkey bones by simmering them in a large pot for 1½ to 2 hours with enough water to cover. Remove bones from pot and set aside to cool. Strain stock with a fine sieve. Measure out about 4 quarts. When bones have cooled, remove whatever meat is on them, cut it into small pieces and add to pot. If the bones don't have much meat on them, add some of the leftover meat. You don't want too much meat in the soup, but just enough so that you have a couple good chunks for each serving. Discard bones.
- Put all ingredients into the pot and cook over low heat for 20 to 30 minutes.
- Serves 10 to 12.

Shchi
(Russian Sauerkraut Soup)

1 ¾ pounds beef (shank, soup meat, or brisket)
¾ pound ham
1 bunch soup greens
8 to 10 cups water
4 to 5 cups sauerkraut,
1 medium onion, chopped
2 cloves garlic
1 tablespoon butter
2 bay leaves
8 black pepper corns
1 tablespoon flour or cornstarch
2 tablespoons water
Salt and black pepper to taste
1 cup sour cream

A note about soup greens: These are a combination of fresh herbs such as parsley, thyme, and dill, and root vegetables such as turnips, carrots, parsley roots, celery roots, and leeks, in any proportion, depending on their availability. A bunch of soup greens will weigh about 1 to 2 pounds.

- Prepare a broth by cooking beef, ham, and soup greens in water. When meat is cooked, strain. Reserve meat and dice. Discard soup greens.
- Squeeze juice from sauerkraut; reserving juice. Briefly cook sauerkraut in boiling water to blanch, then drain and chop.
- Sauté the onion and garlic lightly in butter, then add sauerkraut and cook 10 minutes. Add bay leaves and peppercorns. Add broth and simmer for 45 minutes, until sauerkraut is tender.
- Dissolve flour with in 2 tablespoons of water and add to soup. Simmer for 5 minutes to thicken. Add diced meat and sauerkraut juice to taste. Season with salt and pepper. Continue cooking for 10 minutes.
- Stir in sour cream or add a tablespoon or two to each bowl. Serves 4 to 6.

Sauerkraut Meatball Soup

2 pounds ground beef (can also use pork or chicken)
1 cup fine bread crumbs
2 egg, lightly beaten
1 cup minced onion
½ teaspoon nutmeg
¼ teaspoon salt
3 quarts water
8 cubes chicken bouillon
1 ½ cups evaporated milk
1 cup water
½ cup butter
1 cup white flour
3 cups sauerkraut, with juice

- In a large bowl, combine ground beef, breadcrumbs, eggs, onion, nutmeg, and salt. Using your hands, shape mixture into small balls (or miniature patties for easier browning). Cook meatballs or patties in a large skillet over medium heat until brown.
- In a large stockpot, bring 3 quarts water and bouillon cubes to a boil.
- In a small saucepan, heat milk, water and butter until butter is melted. Place flour in a medium-sized bowl. Whisk a small amount of warm milk mixture into the flour to form a smooth paste; whisk the flour mixture into the remaining warm milk mixture in the saucepan.
- Add everything, including sauerkraut and meatballs, to broth. Bring to a gentle boil and simmer over low heat for 30 minutes, until meatballs are cooked through. Serve hot.
- Serves 8.

Highland Sauerkraut Soup

½ pound ground lamb
2 medium parsnips, chopped
2 10-ounce cans beef broth
2 - 3 cups water
½ cup green onions, chopped
½ teaspoon rosemary
½ cup sauerkraut, drained

- In a large saucepan, brown lamb; drain off access fat. Add parsnips and remaining ingredients and bring to a boil. Reduce heat, cover, and simmer for 30 minutes.

Creamy Reuben Soup

2 cups sauerkraut
½ cup chopped onion
¼ cup chopped celery
¼ cup butter
¼ cup white flour
3 cups water
2 cubes beef bouillon
½ pound corned beef, shredded
3 cups creamilk
5 cups shredded Swiss cheese
6 slices rye or pumpernickel bread, toasted and cut into quarters

- Drain sauerkraut well.
- In a large saucepan, sauté onion and celery in butter until tender. Add flour and cook, stirring, until smooth. Gradually stir in water and bouillon and bring to boil. Reduce heat and simmer, uncovered, for 5 minutes.
- Add corned beef, sauerkraut, creamilk, and 1 cup Swiss cheese. Cook 25-30 minutes, until slightly thickened, stirring frequently.

- Spoon soup into 8 ovenproof bowls. Top each bowl with toasted bread and ½ cup cheese. Place bowls in oven and broil until cheese melts. Serve immediately.
- Serves 8.

Kraut and Vegetable Short Rib Soup

2 pounds beef short ribs
2 pounds soup bones
3 quarts water
2 medium carrots, chopped
2 stalks celery, chopped
6 cups shredded cabbage
3 cups sauerkraut, rinsed and drained
1 medium onion, chopped
3 cloves garlic, chopped
1 14-ounce can diced tomatoes
2 bay leaves
½ tablespoon salt, or to taste
½ teaspoon pepper
4 tablespoons lemon juice
Sugar
1 cup sour cream

- Put beef short ribs and soup bones into a large heavy pot and add water. Bring to a boil. Using a slotted spoon, skim off foam that rises to the top. Reduce heat and simmer, covered, for 2 hours or until meat is tender.
- Remove soup bones from pot and add all remaining ingredients except sour cream. Add more water if necessary. Cover and simmer for 1 to 1 ½ hours, until vegetables are cooked. Serve with a dollop of sour cream in each bowl.

The Day After Soup

3 pounds left-over pork picnic shoulder roast with bone
Water
3 medium potatoes (cut in 1-inch cubes)
2 medium onions (chopped coarsely)
1 - 2 cups sauerkraut
½ teaspoon black pepper

- Trim excess fat off picnic shoulder. Place into a large pot and add water to barely cover. Place lid on pot, slightly askew to allow steam to escape.
- Cook over low heat for 1 to 1 ½ hours, until meat comes off the bone quite easily. Remove from pot and set aside to cool.
- Add potatoes, chopped onions, sauerkraut, and pepper to pot and start cooking over low heat. Meanwhile, remove meat from bone; cut it into 1 to 2-inch chunks, then add them to soup. Cook until potatoes are tender. Add more water if needed. Soup will not suffer too much, but will still remain nice and tangy. Excellent soup. Serves 4 to 5.

Classic Sauerkraut Soup

½ pound smoked pork shank or fresh spare ribs
2 quarts water
1 medium onion, chopped
1 medium potato, diced
1 carrot, diced
½ cup chopped mushrooms
4 cups sauerkraut
1 tablespoon finely chopped onion
1 tablespoon butter
2 tablespoons flour
1 tablespoon sour cream or thick sweet cream
salt and pepper
chopped dill or parsley

- Wash meat; put it into a soup pot and cover with water. Simmer until tender. Add more water if necessary.
- Add onion, potato, and carrot. Continue simmering until vegetables are done.
- Remove meat and press vegetables through a sieve.
- Return the meat and pressed vegetables to the pot, then add the mushrooms and sauerkraut. If kraut is too sour, rinse it in cold water before adding to soup. Simmer these ingredients till the kraut is tender, about 20 minutes.
- Meanwhile, using a small skillet, cook the finely chopped onion in the butter until tender, stir in the flour and brown it lightly. Pour some liquid into it, stir until smooth, and return to soup. Add cream, season to taste, and bring soup to a boil. Flavor with dill or parsley.
- Serve meat as a separate course or place small amounts of it in each bowl of soup. Serve with rye bread.

Sauerkraut Borscht

4 slices medium-lean bacon, chopped
10 cups cold water
4 medium onions, sliced
Small piece of whole ginger, peeled
1 bay leaf
2 cups sauerkraut
Small bunch fresh parsley, chopped
Small bunch of fresh dill weed, chopped
3 medium-sized ripe tomatoes, cut
½ cup sugar

Put water and bacon in medium-sized pot and boil until bacon is almost done. Add sliced onions, ginger, bay leaf, and sauerkraut. Boil for a few minutes. Add remaining ingredients and boil briefly, until tomatoes are just cooked. Serves 8 to 10.

Volga Borscht

½ cup julienned carrot
1 cup thinly sliced onion
1 cup julienned beet
1 tablespoon butter
1 10-ounce can condensed chicken broth
1 cup sauerkraut, rinsed and drained
1 7 ½-ounce can tomato sauce
Sour cream
Grated cucumber

- Put carrots, onion, and beets in a saucepan and add water to cover. Bring to a boil and cook for 20 minutes over low-medium heat.
- Add remaining, except sour cream and cucumber; cook another 5 minutes.
- Serve hot, topped with a dollop of sour cream and a bit of grated cucumber.
- Serves 5.

Hunter's Stew

3 medium-sized dried mushrooms
2 cups water
4 cups sauerkraut
1 apple (peeled, cored, and sliced) or ¼ cup raisins
1 19-ounce can tomatoes
6 peppercorns
2 bay leaves
2 cups diced polish sausage
1 cup chopped bacon
4 potatoes, boiled

- Put mushrooms into a pot, add 2 cups water, and soak for 2 hours. Bring to boil and simmer, covered, for 30 minutes. Remove mushrooms from pot and slice them; put back into water.

- Rinse sauerkraut twice and squeeze it to remove excess water. Add to mushrooms along with the apple or raisins, tomatoes, peppercorns, and bay leaves. Cover and simmer for 30 minutes.
- Add sausage and bacon, adding more water if stew is too thick, and simmer for another 45 minutes.
- Serve with potatoes or rye bread. Sauerkraut is best when allowed to cool, and then reheated before serving.
- Serves 4.

Polish Stew

1 pound Polish sausage, cut in ½-inch slices
Cooking oil
1 ½ pounds stewing beef, cubed
2 small-medium onions, sliced
2 cups mushrooms, sliced
4 cups sauerkraut
1 cut dry white wine
1 10-ounce can tomato sauce.
2 teaspoons soy sauce
1 teaspoon caraway seeds
¼ teaspoon vegetable seasoning

- In a large skillet, sauté sliced sausages for 10 to 15 minutes. Transfer from skillet to a large casserole or roasting pan.
- Heat 1 ½ tablespoons oil in skillet, add beef and brown well on all sides. Transfer to casserole. Sauté onion, adding more oil to skillet as needed; add to casserole.
- Sauté mushrooms with sauerkraut and wine for 5 to 10 minutes. Stir in tomato sauce, soy sauce, caraway seeds, and seasoning. Add to casserole also; mix well. Cover and bake at 350 degrees Fahrenheit for 1 to 1 ½ hours, until meat is tender. Stir casserole every 30 minutes, adding a bit of water if stew gets too dry.
- Serves 8.

Samuel's Beef Stew

2 pounds meaty beef bones
10 cups water
1 pound beef or pork, cut in bit-size pieces
1 medium onion, chopped
3 cloves garlic, chopped
1 tablespoon cooking oil or butter
2 cups sauerkraut, lightly rinsed
1 ½ cups beer
2 - 3 cups cut tomatoes
¾ cup split peas, soaked in hot water for 1 hour
½ teaspoon paprika
½ teaspoon caraway or dill seeds
1 tablespoon parsley
1 tablespoon brown sugar (optional)
2 teaspoons salt, or to taste
1 teaspoon black pepper
½ cup sour cream

- Put beef bones and water into a large stewing pot and bring to a boil. Reduce heat and skim off froth. Simmer for about 1 ½ hours.
- Brown beef or pork in a skillet; add to pot and continue cooking for 30 minutes. Remove bones from pot and set aside to cool.
- Meanwhile, prepare remaining ingredients. Sauté onions and garlic in 1 tablespoon oil for 5 minutes. Add to pot. Remove meat from the bones and cut into bite-size pieces. Add to pot. Stir in all remaining ingredients except sour cream. Continue simmering for about 45 minutes.
- Stir in sour cream before serving.
- Serves 5 to 6.

Krauted Chili

1 tablespoon olive oil
1 pound lean ground beef
1 ½ cups chopped onion
2 or 3 cloves garlic, chopped
1 28-ounce can crushed tomatoes
2 cups sauerkraut
1 14-ounce can pinto beans
1 14-ounce low-sodium beef broth
3 ½ tablespoons chili powder
¼ teaspoon pepper

- Heat oil in a saucepan. Cook onions and garlic briefly over medium. Add meat and cook until browned. Drain. Stir in remaining ingredients. Bring to a boil, then reduce heat to low and simmer, partially covered, for 25 to 30 minutes.
- Serves 4 to 6.

Sauerkraut Salads

Choucroute Froide
(French)

2 tablespoons salad oil
1 cup chopped onion
3 ½ cups sauerkraut
4 whole black peppercorns
1 10-ounce can chicken broth
½ pound back bacon or smoked pork shoulder
2/3 cup white wine
½ cup olive oil
3 tablespoons apple cider vinegar
1 teaspoon salt
¼ teaspoon freshly ground black pepper
½ teaspoon garlic, minced
2 hard-boiled eggs, chopped

- Heat salad oil in a large skillet; sauté onions in oil for 5 minutes. Add sauerkraut, peppercorns, chicken broth, wine, and bacon. Bring to a boil, then cover and cook over low heat for 1 ½ hours, stirring occasionally.
- Remove peppercorns and drain off excess liquid. Refrigerate.
- Before serving, beat together olive oil, apple cider vinegar, salt, pepper, and garlic. Add eggs. Pour mixture over sauerkraut and toss until well blended.
- Serves 6.

Sauerkraut Salad with Yogurt Dressing

2 cups sauerkraut
6 ounces cooked ham, cut in julienne strips
1 ½ cups chopped apples or cut grapes
¼ teaspoon white pepper
¼ teaspoon salt
1 - 1 ½ teaspoons clear honey
2/3 cup plain yogurt

- Rinse and drain sauerkraut; chop coarsely.
- Put all ingredients in a medium-sized bowl in the order given and mix thoroughly. Let sit for 10 to 15 minutes before serving.
- Serves 4.

Crunchy Sauerkraut Salad

2 cups sauerkraut, rinsed and drained
1 small apple, cored and chopped
1/3 cup chopped onion
1/3 cup finely chopped dill pickles
¼ cup olive oil
1 ½ tablespoons lemon juice
1 tablespoon sugar
¼ teaspoon parsley
¼ teaspoon basil
¼ teaspoon dill weed
1/8 teaspoon freshly ground pepper

- Put all ingredients in a bowl; toss to mix well.
- Cover and chill for at least 1 hour.
- Serves 5 to 6.

Fruit and Vegetable Salad

½ cup raisins
2/3 cup mayonnaise
1 tablespoon lemon juice
1 teaspoon sugar
¼ teaspoon salt
3 ½ cups sauerkraut, rinsed and drained
1 ½ cups grated carrots
Lettuce

- Boil raisins in water for 5 minutes; drain and cool.
- Combine mayonnaise, lemon juice, sugar, and salt.
- Put raisins and vegetables (except lettuce) into a salad serving bowl. Add dressing and toss to mix. Serve on lettuce.

Potato Salad with Creamy Sauerkraut Dressing

5 cups cooked sliced potatoes
2 tablespoons chopped onion
¼ teaspoon minced garlic (optional)
¼ cup chopped pimientos
1/3 cup chopped parsley
1/3 cup sauerkraut juice
1 teaspoon salt
1/3 cup skim milk
1/3 cup mayonnaise

- In a bowl, combine potatoes, onions, garlic, pimientos, and parsley. Refrigerate.
- Blend together sauerkraut juice, salt, milk, and mayonnaise. Refrigerate.
- Before serving, pour dressing over potato salad and toss gently to mix
- Serves 8.

Hot Sauerkraut-Potato Salad

4 large potatoes (red-skinned variety)
10 strips medium-lean bacon
¾ cup onion, chopped
1 cup celery, chopped
4 tablespoons flour
1 cup yellow sugar
1 teaspoon salt
½ teaspoon black pepper
2/3 cup apple cider vinegar
2/3 cups water
3 ½ cups sauerkraut, rinsed and drained
1 teaspoon ground mustard
1 small jar pimientos

- Wash potatoes. Cut unpeeled potatoes into quarters and boil until soft, but not mushy. When cool, cut them into 1-inch pieces. Put into a serving bowl.
- Fry bacon in a skillet. When cooked medium-crisp, remove bacon from skillet and place unto a paper towel to drain. Save the drippings. Cut bacon into small pieces.
- Cook the remaining ingredients except the last three in the bacon drippings, until mixture boils and thickens. Add sauerkraut and mustard. Mix well, then pour over potatoes. Gently mix in cut up bacon and the jar of pimento until evenly coated. Serve hot.

Bean and Sauerkraut Salad

¾ cup olive oil
½ cup sugar
1 cup red onion, chopped
2 cups sauerkraut, drained
2 cups cut green beans, cut and steamed
2 cups cut yellow wax beans, cut and steamed
1 cup green peppers, diced
½ cup red peppers, diced
Freshly ground pepper (optional)

- Heat olive oil, sugar, and red onion to simmer. Cool.
- Put sauerkraut, beans (cooled), and peppers into a serving bowl. Pour oil and onion over salad and stir. Add freshly ground pepper, if desired.
- Chill several hours or overnight.
- Serves 8.

Sauerkraut Slaw

½ cup sauerkraut juice
¼ cup sugar
2 cups sauerkraut, finely chopped
1 cup diced onion
1 cup diced green bell pepper

- Pour sauerkraut juice into a small skillet and add sugar. Bring liquid to a boil and cook until sugar is melted.
- In a bowl, combine sauerkraut, onion, and green pepper. Pour the liquid over mixture. Refrigerate before serving.
- Serve with pork roast or meatloaf. Serves 4 to 5.

Sauerkraut Salad

3 ½ cups sauerkraut
1 cup raisins, washed and drained
2 cups chopped celery
Salt and pepper to taste
½ cup apple cider vinegar
1/3 cup olive or grape seed oil
1 cup sugar
¼ cup water

- Lightly rinse sauerkraut and drain well. Put sauerkraut into a serving bowl and add raisins, celery, and seasonings.
- In a small saucepan, mix together the last four ingredients and bring mixture to a boil; stir until sugar is dissolved. Let cool. Pour over salad and refrigerate for 24 hours to marinate.

Sauerkraut Salad

2 cups sauerkraut
1 cup chopped green pepper
1 cup chopped onion, chopped
1 cup chopped celery
½ cup grated carrots
1 ¼ cups sugar
½ cup apple cider vinegar

- Thoroughly rinse sauerkraut and drain.
- Prepare vegetables and mix with sauerkraut.
- Measure sugar and apple cider vinegar into a small saucepan and bring to a boil. Cool.
- Pour cooled vinegar over salad and toss to mix.
- Refrigerate 24 hours before serving.

Sauerkraut Salad

1 cup sauerkraut, rinsed and all liquid squeezed out
1 cup bean sprouts, rinsed with cold water
½ cup finely chopped celery
½ cup chopped green pepper
¼ cup chopped pimientos (optional)
¾ cup whole kernel corn
½ cup chopped green onion
2 tablespoons apple cider vinegar
3 tablespoons clear honey

- In a serving bowl, combine all ingredients except vinegar and honey.
- Combine apple cider vinegar and honey; stir to mix.
- Pour dressing over salad ingredients and toss to mix. Serves 3 to 4.

Sauerkraut and Bacon Salad

1 cup sauerkraut, lightly rinsed and well drained
½ cup julliened carrot
½ cup finely chopped celery
½ cup chopped onion
½ cup chopped green pepper
½ cup chopped red pepper
2 tablespoons white sugar
¼ cup olive oil
6 strips lean bacon

- In a bowl, mix sauerkraut, carrot, celery, onion, and peppers. Combine sugar and olive oil; pour over salad ingredients and toss to mix well. Cover bowl with plastic wrap and place into refrigerator to chill.
- Before serving, cut bacon into ½ pieces and cook in a skillet until crisp. Add bacon bits to salad just before serving. Serves 4.

Krauted Sandwiches, Dogs, and Burgers

Sausage and Kraut Pitas

1 cup chopped onions
1 green bell pepper, seeded and chopped
½ tablespoon olive oil
10 ounces smoked sausages, sliced ¼-inch thick
2 cups sauerkraut, rinsed and drained
½ cup sour cream
2 tablespoons spicy brown mustard
4 60-percent whole-wheat pita breads
2 teaspoons olive oil

- Sauté onions and pepper in skillet with ½ tablespoon olive oil. Add sausage and sauerkraut; heat through. Mix in sour cream and mustard. Heat, but do not boil.
- Cut pita breads in half, crosswise. Spoon equal amounts of mixture in each pita bread half.
- Makes 8 pitas.

Reuben Pita Snacks

2 7-inch (60-percent whole-wheat) pita breads
6 ounces sliced corned beef, chopped
1 cup sauerkraut, rinsed and liquid squeezed out
1/3 cup Thousand Island or Russian salad dressing
2 teaspoons caraway or dill seeds, crushed
1 cup shredded Swiss cheese (mozzarella cheese is fine also)

- Preheat oven to 425 degrees Fahrenheit.
- Separate halves of pita bread by cutting around the edge with a sharp knife.
- Combine corned beef, sauerkraut, salad dressing, and caraway or dill seeds; mix well. Spread evenly on all four pita bread halves. Sprinkle with cheese.
- Place pita breads on a baking sheet and bake in oven for 5 to 7 minutes, until cheese is melted. Makes 4.

Meatloaf Submarine Dagwoods

3 cups sauerkraut, undrained
1 tablespoon brown sugar
¼ cup mayonnaise
¼ cup pickle relish
4 onion buns, split
4 to 8 slices meatloaf, depending on size (cut ¼-inch thick)
2 teaspoons butter
4 slices Swiss cheese

- In a small saucepan, mix sauerkraut and brown sugar and cook about 10 minutes until liquid has been cooked out. Remove from pan and set aside.
- Mix mayonnaise with pickle relish and spread on the onion bun halves.
- Put meatloaf slices and butter in saucepan and heat through, turning once.
- Assemble buns, sandwich style, with hot meat loaf, cheese slices, and hot sauerkraut.
- Serves 4.

Smoked Salmon and Kraut Sandwiches

12 slices rye or pumpernickel bread
¼ cup Russian salad dressing
2 ½ cups sauerkraut, drained
1 pound smoked salmon, sliced
¼ cup butter, softened

- Spread 2 slices rye bread with 1 teaspoon dressing on each slice. Layer bottom bread slice with sauerkraut, salmon, then sauerkraut again. Cover with top bread slice. Repeat with remaining bread slices. Butter outside surfaces of bread and brown both sides in a non-stick surface skillet.
- Makes 6 sandwiches.

Krautwiches

4 hard-boiled eggs
2 cups sauerkraut, with juice squeezed out
½ cup Russian salad dressing
1 medium red onion
6 onion buns
8 ounces thinly sliced salami or corned beef
6 slices Muenster cheese
6 ounces sliced liverwurst
6 lettuce leaves

- In a small bowl, mash one egg with a fork and stir in sauerkraut and salad dressing. Chop half of the onion and add to sauerkraut mixture. Slice the remaining eggs and onion. Set aside.
- Split buns and place equal amounts of salami, cheese, liverwurst, lettuce, sliced onion and sauerkraut mixture on bottoms. Top with sliced eggs. Replace tops of buns and serve.
- Serves 6.

Smoked Turkey Reuben Sandwiches

1/3 cup sauerkraut
3 tablespoons Thousand Island or Russian salad dressing
2 slices smoked turkey
2 slices Swiss cheese
4 slices dark rye bread
4 tablespoons butter

- Rinse sauerkraut and squeeze out all the juice.
- Spread dressing on bread slices. Arrange turkey, cheese, and sauerkraut on two of the rye bread slices. Place remaining slices on top.
- Melt butter over medium heat. Place sandwich in the skillet and brown on both sides.
- Garnish with sliced pickles and apples.
- Makes 2 sandwiches. To make more, multiply ingredients.

Reuben Fish Sandwich

1 can flaked tuna or salmon (or equivalent fresh - about 1 cup)
½ cup well drained sauerkraut
¼ cup chopped dill pickles
¼ cup mayonnaise
1 tablespoon horseradish or minced garlic-ginger spread
6 - 8 slices rye bread, depending on size
6 - 8 slices Swiss cheese
2 - 3 tablespoons butter

- If using fresh fish, bake, broil, or poach, then cool and flake. Mix fish, sauerkraut, pickles, mayonnaise, and horseradish. Proportion mixture evenly on 3 to 4 slices of bread. Top each slice with 2 slices of cheese, then top with remaining bread. Melt butter in skillet. Place sandwiches in skillet and grill on each side until golden brown.
- Makes 3 large sandwiches or 4 smaller ones.

Reuben Pizza Bagels

4 rye or multigrain bagels
1 pound corned beef
2 cups sauerkraut, rinsed and drained
8 thinly cut tomato slices
4 tablespoons sweet pickle relish
8 slices Swiss cheese

- Preheat oven to 400 degrees Fahrenheit.
- Cut bagels in half. Divide corned beef among 8 bagel halves.
- Combine sauerkraut and relish. Mix. Divide and mound on top of corned beef. Top with tomato slices. Place one slice of Swiss cheese on each bagel half.
- Bake in oven for about 5 minutes, until bagels are hot and cheese is melted. Serves 4.

Oktoberfest Kraut Sandwiches

¼ cup butter
1 large onion, finely chopped
1 medium tart apple, peeled, cored, and chopped
4 cups sauerkraut, rinsed and drained
1 tablespoon caraway or dill seeds, crushed
½ cup spicy brown mustard
12 English muffins, split and toasted
2 pounds bratwurst, cooked or fried, then sliced horizontally
16 slices Swiss cheese, about 1 pound
Paprika

- In a skillet, melt the butter. Add the onion and apple; sauté lightly. Stir in the sauerkraut and caraway or dill seeds. Cook to heat through.
- Spread mustard on muffins, then top with bratwurst slices. Divide the sauerkraut mixture evenly over bratwurst. Top each with Swiss cheese.
- Set oven to broil; place sandwiches onto jellyroll pans or cookie sheets and broil until cheese melts. Sprinkle with paprika and serve. Serves 12.

Salmon Kraut Club Sandwiches

12 1-ounce thinly sliced salmon filets
½ cup brown Dijon Mustard
Olive oil
1 tablespoon chopped fresh dill weed
8 strips bacon
1 small onion, sliced
1 cup sauerkraut, rinsed and drained
1 medium tomato, cut in 8 ¼-inch slices
Salt and pepper, to taste
12 slices light rye bread
Tartar sauce

- Put salmon fillets, mustard, ½ cup olive oil, and dill into a large bowl or casserole; marinate in refrigerator for several hours.
- In a skillet, fry bacon over medium heat until semi-crisp. Remove bacon from pan, reserving 2 tablespoons of the bacon drippings. Set bacon aside. Sauté onion in bacon drippings until translucent. Stir in sauerkraut. Cook, stirring, until heated through. Remove from skillet and set aside.
- In the skillet, sauté salmon fillets over medium heat in some olive oil until cooked.
- Drizzle tomato slices with olive oil; season to taste with salt and pepper.
- Lay two tomato slices and two strips of bacon on a slice of rye bread. Top with some of the tarter sauce. Cover with second slice of bread. Layer sauerkraut, salmon, and additional tartar sauce over bread. Place third slice of bread on top. Cut club sandwich style.
- Repeat with remaining bread slices and sandwich ingredients.
- Makes 4 sandwiches.

Reuben Sandwiches

8 slices corned beef
2 slices Swiss cheese
4 slices dark rye or pumpernickel bread
½ cup sauerkraut, rinsed and drained
4 - 6 tablespoons Thousand Island or French dressing
4 tablespoons butter

- Place two slices of the corned beef and 1 slice of the Swiss cheese on each of two pieces of rye or pumpernickel bread. Heap equal amount of sauerkraut on each. Spread dressing on sauerkraut. Place remaining slices of corned beef over top, then top with remaining slices of bread.
- Melt butter in skillet over medium heat. Grill sandwich on both sides until golden brown. Serve warm. Makes 2 sandwiches.

Reuben Pita Sandwiches

4 7-inch pitas
1/3 cup mayonnaise
1 ½ tablespoons brown prepared mustard
¾ teaspoon caraway seeds
1 12-ounce can cooked corned beef
2 cups shredded Swiss or mozzarella cheese
1 ½ cups sauerkraut, rinsed and thoroughly drained

- Cut pitas in half crosswise, forming two pockets from each.
- In large bowl, combine mayonnaise, mustard, and caraway seeds. Stir in corned beef, cheese, sauerkraut, and Russian salad dressing, mixing well. Spoon into pita halves.
- Heat in the microwave on high for 1 minute, until cheese begins to melt and filling is hot.
- Makes 8 pita sandwiches.

Variation: To make a handy snacks or appetizers with the same filling as above, spread some filling (¼-inch thick) on 6-inch soft corn tortillas. Place tortillas on a cooking sheet and bake in a preheated 425-degree Fahrenheit oven for 5 to 7 minutes, until cheese is melted. When done, cut each tortilla into 4 to 6 wedges with a pizza-cutting wheel. Makes an excellent appetizer. You may need to divide the ingredients above, as the recipe would be too large for regular use, unless you are looking to serve a large crowd.

Fine Liver and Sauerkraut Sandwiches

¼ cup fine processed liver sausage
½ cup sauerkraut, rinsed and squeezed dry
1 ½ tablespoons finely chopped green onions
1 tablespoon Russian salad dressing
½ teaspoon prepared brown mustard
2/3 cup shredded Swiss or mozzarella cheese
4 slices light rye bread
4 tablespoons butter

- This fine liver sausage is actually more like a thick paste. You can purchase it in most superstores.
- In a bowl, combine liver sausage, sauerkraut, green onions, dressing, and mustard. Using a fork, mash sausage, blending all ingredients together.
- Spread equal amounts of mixture on two slices of rye bread. Top with cheese. Top with remaining bread slices.
- Melt butter in a skillet over medium heat. Grill sandwiches on both sides until golden brown. Serve warm.
- Makes 2 sandwiches.

Corned Beef Special

4 slices rye or pumpernickel bread
Mustard (for unique variation, you may substitute with vegemite yeast spread)
3 ½ cups sauerkraut, drained
1 to 1 ½ pounds cooked corned beef
8 sliced Swiss cheese
12 tomato slices

- Spread bread with mustard and top with corned beef and sauerkraut. Top each with 2 slices of Swiss cheese. Put slices on a baking sheet and broil in oven just until cheese is melted. Top with tomato slices and serve.
- Serves 4.

Krauted Chicken Sandwich

4 strips cold chicken breast (or use use turkey)
½ cup sauerkraut, well rinsed and drained
Thinly sliced onion
Freshly ground black pepper, to taste
Mayonnaise
Prepared mustard (optional)
2 slices whole-wheat or rye bread (toasted, if preferred)

- Place the chicken, sauerkraut, and onion in layers on one slice of bread. Season with Pepper to taste. Spread desired amount of Mayonnaise and mustard on remaining bread slice and place on top of chicken, sauerkraut, and onion.
- Serves 1.

Reuben Turnovers

2 cups Bisquick
½ to 2/3 cup cold water
5 ounces thinly sliced smoked corned beef
1 cup sauerkraut, drained
¼ cup Thousand Island dressing
1 cup shredded Swiss cheese
2 tablespoons butter, melted
Caraway or poppy seeds

- Preheat oven to 400 degrees Fahrenheit.
- Mix Bisquick and water. Quickly knead into a soft dough, then into a ball on a floured cloth covered board. Roll the dough out into a 12x18-inch rectangle. Cut rectangle into 6 squares. Layer corned beef over triangular half of each square.
- Mix sauerkraut, dressing, and cheese; spoon over corned beef. Fold dough over sauerkraut mixture, forming a triangle. Press the edges with a floured fork to seal. Brush tops with butter; sprinkle with caraway or poppy seeds. Bake on an ungreased cookie sheet at 400 degrees Fahrenheit for about 20 minutes, until golden brown. Serves 6.

Kraut Crescent Dogs

1 8-ounce can Pillsbury crescent dough
¾ cup sauerkraut, drained
(8) ¼ -inch slices Swiss cheese
8 wieners

- Preheat oven to 375 degrees Fahrenheit.
- Unroll dough according to instructions on can and separate into 8 triangles. Slit wieners to ½ inch from ends and place cheese in slits. Place wiener at wide end of dough. Put some sauerkraut (1 to 1 ½ tablespoons) on dough and roll up.
- Place crescent dogs on an ungreased baking sheet. Bake for 10 to 13 minutes. Serve warm. Makes 8.

Sauerkraut Swiss Dogs

2 cups sauerkraut, with juice
1 teaspoon basil
8 hotdog buns, split
8 slices Swiss cheese
8 large beef wieners

- In a saucepan or skillet, combine sauerkraut and basil. Cover and cook over low heat for about 10 minutes, stirring occasionally. Drain off excess juice.
- Cut slits in each frankfurter (without cutting all the way through); broil about 7 inches from source of heat 3 to 5 minutes. Turn and broil 3 minute longer.
- Place Swiss cheese on bun bottoms and broil about 7 inches from source of heat 3 to 5 minutes until cheese is melted and lightly browned.
- Place wieners on bun bottoms. Top with sauerkraut and bun tops.
- Serves 8.

Classic Hot-dogs with Sauerkraut

10 wieners (about 1 pound)
2 cups sauerkraut
10 wiener buns, buttered
Prepared yellow mustard
Ketchup (if preferred)
Chopped onion

- In a saucepan, heat water to the boiling point. Drop wieners into water; reduce heat. Cover saucepan and simmer for about 7 minutes.
- In a small skillet, heat sauerkraut over low heat; drain.
- Serve wieners in buns, topped with sauerkraut, mustard, ketchup (if preferred), and chopped onion.

Hot-dogs with Kraut and Apples

6 large wieners
1 ½ cups apple juice
3 cups sauerkraut
2 medium unpeeled Red Delicious apples, cored
6 whole-wheat hamburger buns, halved

- Slit wieners 4 times diagonally, cutting about ¾ of the way through.
- In a skillet, heat apple juice to a simmer. Add wieners and cook 5 to 7 minutes, until wieners curl. Remove from skillet. Add sauerkraut and cook until most of the juice is absorbed. At that point, cut six slices from the center of the apples and set aside. Finely chop the remaining apple pieces; stir into the sauerkraut. Place cooked wieners on top of the sauerkraut and continue simmering until all the juice is absorbed.
- Place an apple slice on each of the bottom bun halves. Place wieners on top of apple slices and top with sauerkraut and apple mixture. Place remaining bun halves over top and serve.
- Serves 6.

Confetti Sauerkraut and Wieners

1 small onion, chopped
1 tablespoon butter
2 cups sauerkraut, drained
¼ cup raisins
1/3 cup grated carrot
½ cup apple juice
8 large beef wieners
8 hotdog buns

- In a saucepan or skillet, sauté onion in butter until soft. Mix in sauerkraut, raisins, carrot, and apple juice. Bring to a boil, then cover and simmer for 15 minutes.
- Cook wieners however you prefer. Place wieners in hotdog buns; top with sauerkraut mixture. Serves 8.

Reuben Burgers

1 ½ pounds ground beef
1 cup corned beef, chopped
1 cup onions, finely chopped
1 tablespoon Worcestershire sauce
¼ teaspoon garlic salt
½ teaspoon salt
1/8 teaspoon black pepper
1/8 teaspoon cayenne pepper
1 cup sauerkraut, drained
6 slices Swiss cheese (¼ inch thick, 3 by 3 inches square)

- Mix together all the ingredients except the sauerkraut and Swiss cheese.
- Shape mixture into 6 patties, each about ¾-inch thick, and place them on a baking pan. Set oven control to broil or 500 degrees Fahrenheit. Put the pan on the top rack of the oven and broil them, turning once, for 12 to 15 minutes.
- Top each patty with sauerkraut and a cheese slice. Broil until the cheese is melted and has a light brown color.
- Serve on toasted rye or pumpernickel buns or bread.
- Serves 6.

Krauted Barbecue Burgers

2 cups sauerkraut, drained
½ cup whole-berry cranberry sauce
½ cup barbecue sauce
¼ cup brown sugar
2 eggs
½ cup water
2 packages dry onion soup mix
2 pounds ground beef
8 burger buns, split and toasted

- In a large saucepan, combine sauerkraut, cranberry sauce, and sugar. Simmer for 15 to 20 minutes, stirring occasionally.
- Meanwhile, beat eggs and add water and soup mix. Let stand for 3 minutes, then add beef and mix lightly.
- Form 8 beef patties. Grill on barbecue, uncovered, at medium-hot setting for about 6 minutes, then turn and grill another 4 to 6 minutes, or until meat is no longer pink.
- Place patties on bun bottoms, top with the warm sauce and replace bun tops.
- Serves 8.

Turkey or Chicken Kraut Burgers

1 pound lean ground turkey or chicken
2 cups sauerkraut, lightly rinsed, and squeezed dry, divided
¾ cup chopped green onions, divided
1 tablespoon finely chopped pimientos
1 egg white, beaten
2 tablespoons prepared mustard
½ cup shredded cheddar, mozzarella, or Swiss cheese

- Combine turkey or chicken, 1 cup sauerkraut, ½ cup green onions, pimientos, egg white and mustard. Shape into 3 to 4-inch patties. Place oven rack on top level, about 6 inches from heat. Place patties on a baking sheet and broil for 11 to 13 minutes, or until meat is no longer pink, turning patties over once.
- Combine remaining sauerkraut, onions, and the cheese. Top patties with mixture. Broil 3 to 5 minutes, or until cheese melts. Serve with hamburger buns.
- Serves 6.

Sauerkraut Sidedish Entrees

Kraut Goulash for Noodles and Dumplings

4 slices bacon, finely chopped
¾ pound pork tenderloin, cut in 1-inch pieces
2/3 cup chopped onion
1 teaspoon caraway seeds
1 tablespoon paprika
1 10-ounce can condensed chicken stock
2 cups water
2 ½ cups sauerkraut, rinsed and drained
½ cup chopped green bell pepper
½ cup chopped tomato
½ cup sour cream
2 tablespoons flour
Salt and pepper to taste
Hot cooked noodles or dumplings
Fresh chopped parsley (optional)

- In a large, heavy, deep skillet or Dutch Oven, cook bacon until crisp. Remove from pan and crumble in small bits; set aside. Leave bacon drippings in pan.
- Put pork, onion, caraway seeds, and paprika into pan and cook, stirring, until meat is well browned. Stir in chicken stock, water and sauerkraut. Cover and simmer for about 1 hour.
- Add green pepper and tomato; continue simmering for 30 minutes, stirring occasionally. Combine sour cream and flour. Stir mixture into goulash over higher heat and cook, stirring, until thickened. Add salt and pepper to taste. Ladle over noodles or dumplings. Garnish with bacon and sprinkle with fresh chopped parsley if preferred.
- Serves 4.

Colcannon Dish
(Irish and Scottish)

3 pounds red-skinned potatoes, peeled and quartered
¼ cup minced onion
2 cloves garlic, minced
¾ cup sour cream
½ cup butter, melted
1 ½ cups sauerkraut, drained
1 cup grated Monterey Jack, Gouda, or Muenster cheese
Salt and pepper to taste

- Cook or steam potatoes until very soft. Drain. Put potatoes in a large mixing bowl and mash thoroughly.
- Add onion, garlic, sour cream, and butter. Beat with a whisk until smooth. Gently stir in sauerkraut; season to taste with salt and pepper.
- Put mixture in a greased 2-quart casserole. Top with cheese. Bake in 350-degree Fahrenheit oven for 35 to 45 minutes.
- Serves 6.

Potatoes Paris

3 ½ cups sauerkraut
3 tablespoons cooking oil
1 small onion
6 cups mashed potatoes
1 egg, beaten
Paprika
Butter

- Rinse Sauerkraut and drain.
- Sauté chopped onion in oil for two minutes. Add sauerkraut and cook for 12 to 15 minutes over medium low heat.

- Grease a casserole and place 3 cups mashed potatoes on the bottom. Add sauerkraut and top with remaining potatoes. Brush top with beaten egg, sprinkle with paprika and dot with butter.
- Bake in a 350-degree Fahrenheit oven for 30 to 45 minutes.

Sauerkraut in Sour Cream

6 cups sauerkraut
1 10-ounce can chicken or beef consommé
½ cup onions, chopped
1 teaspoon cooking oil or butter
1 ½ cups sour cream
A few sprigs parsley
2 tart apples, peeled, cored, and sliced

- In a large saucepan, cook sauerkraut and consommé, uncovered, for 20 to 30 minutes until consommé is almost cooked out.
- Meanwhile, using a small skillet, brown onions lightly in oil or butter. Remove from skillet and add sour cream and parsley. Scald (heat just to boiling point, then remove from heat).
- Stir onions, sour cream, and apples into sauerkraut and heat through before serving.
- Serve with roast pork, chops, or ribs.

Christmas Eve Peas and Sauerkraut Dish
(Ukrainian)

2/3 cup dried split peas
3 cups sauerkraut, rinsed, and drained
1 cup water
¾ cup finely chopped salt pork or bacon
1 cup chopped onion
Sauerkraut juice
3 tablespoons flour
¾ cup sliced mushrooms
2 cloves garlic, crushed
¼ teaspoon black pepper
1 teaspoon salt, or to taste
3 tablespoons sour cream

- Soak the peas overnight. When ready to cook, add 4 cups lightly salted water; bring to a boil, then reduce heat and simmer until peas are tender. Drain and set aside.
- Put sauerkraut in a saucepan and add 1 cup water. Cook over low heat for about 20 minutes. Drain any remaining liquid.
- Preheat oven to 350 degrees Fahrenheit.
- In a large skillet, cook salt pork or bacon until almost crisp. Remove from pan and set aside. Reserve 3 tablespoons of the drippings in the skillet; sauté the chopped onions until just soft. Combine the flour with a bit of sauerkraut juice and stir to mix. Add to skillet and cook, while stirring, adding more juice as needed to make a smooth gravy.
- Put all ingredients into a casserole and bake in oven for about 30 minutes.
- Serves 6.

Tyrolean Dumplings with Hot Sauerkraut

1 tablespoon finely chopped onion or chives
1 tablespoon chopped parsley
½ cup butter
1 loaf day-old bread, diced
1 ½ - 2 cups milk
2 eggs, slightly beaten
Salt to taste
2/3 cup flour
Hot sauerkraut

- Using a heavy frying pan, sauté onion and parsley in butter until crisp and golden. Add diced bread and place all in a bowl. Mix milk, eggs, and salt. Pour over bread. Blend in flour, as needed, to form a soft batter.
- Drop by rounded tablespoonfuls into gently boiling salted water and cook over low heat for 12 to 15 minutes.
- When done, remove from water with a slotted spoon, sprinkle with paprika and serve over hot sauerkraut.

Cornmeal Dumplings with Hot Sauerkraut

1 cup cornmeal
¼ cup white flour
1 teaspoon baking powder
½ teaspoon salt
2 eggs, beaten
½ cup milk
1 tablespoon butter, melted
Stock (corned beef, consommé, or any clear soup stock)

- In a medium-sized bowl, mix dry ingredients. In a small bowl combine eggs, milk and melted butter. Pour into dry mixture and mix only until dry ingredients are moistened.
- Drop batter by rounded tablespoons into gently boiling stock, cover, and cook over low heat for 15 minutes.
- Serve over hot sauerkraut.

Applesauce Sauerkraut

4 cups sauerkraut, rinsed and drained
2 cups sweetened applesauce
½ teaspoon caraway seeds
1 tablespoon butter

- Mix all ingredients. Place in a greased casserole dish and bake at 375 degrees Fahrenheit for 30 to 45 minutes.
- Serves 6.

Kraut and Pork Egg Rolls

1 pound pork sausage meat
1 cup chopped onions
½ cup finely chopped celery
½ cup coarsely grated carrots
1 ½ cups sauerkraut, drained
2 tablespoons soy sauce
½ teaspoon sugar
¼ teaspoon pepper
1 16-ounce package egg roll wrappers
Cooking oil or shortening, for frying

- In a large skillet, cook sausage meat with onions, celery, and carrots until sausage meat is well browned and vegetables are tender-crisp.
- In a large bowl, combine sausage and vegetable mixture, sauerkraut, soy sauce, sugar, and pepper; mix well.
- Place ¼ cup filling in center of egg roll wrapper. Fold one corner over filling then roll up, tucking in the sides as you roll. Moisten final corner with water and press edges to seal.
- In a large saucepan or electric frying kettle, heat oil to 375 degrees Fahrenheit. Deep-fry several egg rolls at a time for 3 to 4 minutes or until golden brown and crispy. Place on paper towels to drain.
- Makes 20 egg rolls.

Potato Sauerkraut Casserole

6 strips bacon
2 cups sauerkraut
1 ½ pounds peeled and cubed (½ to ¾-inch) potatoes
½ cup spicy brown Dijon mustard
¼ teaspoon black pepper

- Chop bacon and cook in a skillet until crisp. Drain, reserving 3 tablespoons drippings.
- Put all ingredients, along with bacon drippings, into a casserole dish; mix well.
- Put casserole into the oven and bake at 350 degrees Fahrenheit for 1 hour, or until potatoes are tender. To ensure even cooking throughout, stir every 15 minutes.
- Serve with meat dish of your choice and a salad.
- Serves 3 to 4.

Crockpot Kraut

4 cups sauerkraut, rinsed and drained
1 small head of cabbage, thinly sliced (about 1/8-inch)
1 medium onion, finely chopped
2 medium apples, peeled, cored, and finely chopped
2 teaspoons caraway seeds
2 ½ tablespoons white sugar
2 ½ tablespoons brown sugar
¼ cup bacon drippings

- In a large crockpot, layer the sauerkraut with sliced cabbage, onion, and apples. Sprinkle each layer with caraway seeds and sugars. Pour bacon drippings over top.
- Put cover on crockpot and cook on low for 8 to 10 hours, or about 3 hours on high setting. Stir well before serving. Serve with roast pork or duck, along with potatoes.
- Serves about 10.

Sauerkraut Dumplings

1 pound peeled and quartered potatoes
1 cup sauerkraut
5 strips bacon
2/3 cup fine breadcrumbs
¼ cup onions, minced
1 egg, beaten
¼ teaspoon salt
¼ teaspoon pepper
¾ to 1 cup flour

- Put potatoes into a saucepan and cook until soft. Remove from pan; mash and set aside to cool off for handling.
- Lightly rinse sauerkraut; squeeze out all the juice and chop. Set aside.
- Put bacon in a skillet and cook over medium-high heat until crisp. Remove from skillet and lay on a paper towel to drain, then chop finely. Combine bacon bits with breadcrumbs and set aside.
- Drain off all but 2 teaspoons of bacon drippings from skillet; add onions and sauté over medium heat until soft.
- Pour 8 cups water into a small pot or large saucepan. Add 1 teaspoon salt. Bring water to a slow boil over medium heat.
- Combine all ingredients and mix well in a large mixing bowl, adding ¾ to 1 cup flour so that the dumplings are just slightly sticky and you can form dumplings using hands. Make dumplings about 1 ½ inches in diameter. Place dumplings gently into boiling water and boil gently for 10 to 15 minutes until cooked through. When done, remove dumplings with a slotted spoon and roll them in the bacon bits and breadcrumbs to coat.
- Serve with meat dish of your choice.
- Serves 4.

Stewed Kraut

2 cups shredded fresh cabbage
½ cup water
2 cups sauerkraut, with juice
¼ tablespoon brown sugar
3 tablespoons butter
3 tablespoons flour

- Place fresh cabbage into a saucepan. Add ½ cup water. Cover, bring to a boil, and cook over low heat for 30 to 40 minutes, until cabbage is soft. Add sauerkraut and brown sugar. Add a bit more water if necessary (¼ inch of juice on the bottom is about right). Simmer for another 10 minutes to blend.
- In the meantime, prepare a brown sauce: Melt the butter in a small skillet and add the flour; cook over medium heat, while stirring, until sauce is a rich brown. Strain sauce into kraut to remove lumps; stir to mix.
- Serve as a vegetable side dish. Serves 4.

Paprika Sauerkraut

1 large onion, chopped
1 tablespoon butter
1 tablespoon flour
3 ½ cups sauerkraut
2 teaspoons paprika
1 10-ounce can tomato soup
2 tablespoons sugar
2 cups water
1 teaspoon garlic powder (optional)

- In a saucepan, brown onions in butter. Add flour and blend well. Combine with remaining ingredients and simmer over low heat for about an hour.
- Serves 4.

Savory Sauerkraut

2 pounds sauerkraut
½ pound bacon, cut in 1-inch pieces
4 tablespoons unsalted butter
¾ cup carrot julienne
1 ½ cups onions, sliced
½ cup chopped parsley
8 peppercorns
2 bay leaves
1 ½ cups dry white wine
3 cups chicken or beef stock, or more if needed
Salt to taste
1 pound knockwurst
1 pound bratwurst

- Thoroughly rinse sauerkraut and squeeze out all the liquid.
- Using a medium-sized skillet, simmer bacon in one cup water for 10 minutes; drain.
- Melt butter over medium heat in a large non-aluminum casserole or Dutch oven. Add bacon, carrots, and onions; cook over low heat for 10 minutes. Stir in sauerkraut and cook an additional 10 minutes. Add parsley, peppercorns, bay leaves, wine, and stock. Mix well; add salt to taste.
- Preheat the oven to 300 degrees Fahrenheit.
- Lightly grease a piece of waxed paper that will fit over the sauerkraut; place greased side down in pan and press down to cover well. Bring to a simmer, cover, and bake in the oven for 3 to 3 ½ hours
- Using the tip of a sharp knife, prick sausages or make small cuts. Brown lightly in the skillet; drain fat. Remove cover and waxed paper from casserole and add sausages to casserole, laying them on top of kraut. Continue to cook in the oven, uncovered, for another 30 minutes or until sausages are cooked and liquid is absorbed.
- Serves 6.

Pannonian Style Sauerkraut Dish

2 pounds sauerkraut
2 bay leaves
4 juniper berries
4 black peppercorns
4 pimientos
½ teaspoon caraway seeds
¼ cup butter
2 medium onions, chopped
2 tablespoons sugar
½ cup white wine
1 tablespoon Hungarian paprika
1 cup sour cream
salt to taste

- Taste the sauerkraut, and if too sour for your taste, rinse with cold water.
- Place sauerkraut in a large saucepan. Add water to cover. Add bay leaves, juniper berries, peppercorns, pimientos, and caraway seeds. Cook until sauerkraut is tender; drain.
- In a skillet, sauté onions in butter until yellow. Add sugar and cook until well browned and caramelized. Add the wine and stir.
- Add onions to sauerkraut; mix well.
- Mix together sour cream and paprika until smooth; stir into sauerkraut.
- Heat quickly, adding salt if needed, and serve. Serve with meat dish of your choice.
- Serves 4 to 6.

Sauerkraut with Pineapple

3 cups sauerkraut, thoroughly rinsed and squeezed dry
2 ½ cups unsweetened pineapple juice
1 19-ounce can pineapple bits (or rings, cut into chunks)

- In a large saucepan, bring sauerkraut and pineapple juice to a boil over high heat, stirring as it heats. Reduce heat to low; simmer, covered, for 1 hour or until most of the liquid has been absorbed by the sauerkraut.
- Stir the pineapple bits into the cooked sauerkraut, cook for two minutes, then pour the entire mixture into a large sieve set over a bowl. When all the liquid has drained off, transfer sauerkraut and pineapple to a serving dish or onto a plate.
- Serve with pork roast, roast duck, or any roasted game birds. Serves 6.

Sauerkraut with Wine and Grapes

4 cups sauerkraut, thoroughly rinsed and drained
1 ¼ cups dry white wine
1 ½ tablespoons bacon drippings
1 cup seedless green grapes

- In a heavy skillet or saucepan, heat the bacon drippings over medium heat. Add sauerkraut and cook for about 7 minutes, separating the strands with a fork. Add wine; bring to a boil, then reduce heat to low. Simmer, covered, for 45 to 60 minutes or until most of the wine has been absorbed by the sauerkraut.
- Stir in the grapes and simmer, covered, for 10 minutes longer until the grapes are cooked, but not mushy.
- Transfer sauerkraut to a serving bowl. Serve as a side dish with pork roast, pork chops, duck, or wild game birds.
- Serves 4.

Potato Roulade with Sauerkraut

1 pound peeled potatoes
1 ½ cups sauerkraut
¼ teaspoon black pepper
Salt to taste
1 medium onion, chopped
¼ pound bacon, finely chopped
4 eggs
1 - 1 ½ cups flour
1 cup sour cream
Butter or lard

- Boil or steam potatoes until very soft. Remove from pot and cool.
- Meanwhile, place sauerkraut into a small skillet or saucepan; add a bit of water and season with salt and pepper. Cover and simmer for 15 minutes.
- Meanwhile, in another skillet, sauté onions and bacon just until the bacon turns slightly crispy. Drain off excess fat.
- Drain sauerkraut and mix in bacon and onion.
- Put potatoes into a medium-sized mixing bowl and mash. Beat eggs and add to potatoes, mixing well. Add flour and form very soft dough that's just barely past the sticky stage. Roll dough out on a well-floured board and pat into a 10x14-inch rectangle.
- Spread sauerkraut and bacon filling evenly on top of dough to within 1 inch of edges. Roll up dough and filling like a jellyroll. Brush roulade with melted butter or lard. Transfer to a well-greased baking pan and bake in a 350 degree Fahrenheit oven for 30 minutes. To prevent pastry from burning, make sure the rack is situated in the middle of the oven - not too close to either the top or the bottom.
- When done, let cool slightly, then cut into ¾-inch slices. Serve with sour cream as an appetizer or as an addition to meat dishes of your choice.
- Serves 6.

Sauerkraut Veal Goulash

2 pounds veal
2 tablespoons oil
2 onions, sliced
2 cloves garlic
2 medium tomatoes, peeled and quartered
Black pepper
¼ teaspoon paprika
1 cup sour cream
3 ½ cups sauerkraut

- Cut veal into 1-inch cubes.
- Using a large heavy skillet or saucepan, brown onions and garlic in oil. Add veal and brown on all sides. Add tomatoes and season with pepper and paprika. Add water to cover. Cover pan and simmer for 1 ½ hours. Strain. Simmer liquid gently to reduce amount. Add sour cream and simmer for about 4 minutes.
- Pour the sauce over the meat and heat through.
- Serve with heated sauerkraut. Serves 8.

Barbecued Sauerkraut

½ cup chopped onion
5 strips bacon, chopped
1 14-ounce can tomatoes, diced
2 cups sauerkraut, well-drained
3/4 cup brown sugar
1 tablespoon butter
8 ounces Ukrainian garlic sausage, diced

- In a skillet, sauté onion with bacon.
- Put onion and bacon into a casserole dish; add sauerkraut, tomatoes, brown sugar, and butter. Mix well.
- Put casserole into oven and bake, uncovered, for 1 to 1 ½ hours at 350 degrees Fahrenheit. When done, casserole should have slight caramel-like edges, but not burnt.
- Serve with potatoes or pasta dish of your choice.
- Serves 6.

Sauerkraut Main Course Entrees

Pork Chops with Sauerkraut and Mushroom Gravy

6 pork chops (2 - 2 ½ pounds)
1 10-ounce can Cream of Mushroom & Garlic Soup
2 cups sauerkraut
1 - 2 tablespoons balsamic vinegar (optional)
¼ teaspoon caraway seeds
1/8 teaspoon black pepper
2 teaspoons parsley

Note: These chops are tasty enough without the balsamic vinegar, but the vinegar brings a subtle tangy flavor to the chops.

- In a large roasting pan, mix together mushroom soup, sauerkraut (don't rinse unless you prefer less of a sour flavor), balsamic vinegar, caraway seeds, pepper, and parsley.
- Place chops and other ingredients in pan and flip a few times to make sure the chops are well covered with all the ingredients.
- Put roasting pan in the oven and bake for about 30 minutes at 350 degrees Fahrenheit.
- Serve with mashed, cooked, baked, or fried potatoes, some applesauce, and a salad of your choice. Serves 4.

Pork Chops Warsaw

6 pork chops (½ inch thick)
2 medium onions, chopped
2 cloves garlic
¼ cup butter
1 ½ cups boiling water
Salt and black pepper
2 bay leaves
3 ½ cups sauerkraut
3 medium apples, peeled, cored, and chopped
3 tablespoons pearl barley
1 ½ teaspoons caraway seeds

- Using a large skillet, melt butter; brown pork chops, onion and garlic. Add water, salt, pepper, and bay leaves. Simmer for 20 minutes. Add sauerkraut, apple, pearl barley, and caraway seeds. Cook over low heat until meat is tender, about 1 hour. Serves 4 to 5.

Sauerkraut with Potatoes and Smoked Pork Loin Chops

2 medium-large potatoes, peeled and sliced
3 cups sauerkraut, rinsed and drained
1 medium apple, peeled, cored, and chopped
1 ½ tablespoons prepared mustard
¼ teaspoon dill or caraway seed
½ cup apple juice or apple cider
2 pounds boneless smoked pork loin chops

- Arrange potato slices in a lightly greased 12x7x2-inch baking dish.
- Mix together sauerkraut, apple, mustard, and caraway seeds. Spread over potatoes. Pour apple juice or apple cider over. Arrange pork chops on top. Bake, covered with a lid or foil, at 350 degrees Fahrenheit for about 1 hour.
- Serves 4.

Pork Chops with Sauerkraut

2 slices bacon, diced
1 medium onion, chopped
2 tart green apples, peeled, cored, and chopped
5 cups sauerkraut, rinsed and drained
¼ teaspoon cumin
1/8 teaspoon caraway seeds (optional)
3 to 4 juniper berries
½ cup dry white wine
1/3 cup water
1 tablespoon lard or oil
1 ½ - 2 pounds pork chops (smoked or plain)

- Cook bacon, onion, and apple in a large heavy skillet over medium heat until onion is soft. Add sauerkraut, cumin, caraway seeds (if preferred) juniper berries, wine, and water. Cook, uncovered for 10 minutes.
- Meanwhile melt lard in another (small) skillet. Quickly brown each pork chop on both sides. Arrange pork chops on top of sauerkraut in the large skillet, cover, and simmer for 1 hour.
- Serve with rye bread or potatoes. Serves 4 to 5.

Braised Pork Chops with Sauerkraut # 1

6 pork chops (1-inch thick)
2 tablespoons flour
Salt
Freshly ground black pepper
3 tablespoons shortening
2 cups sauerkraut
6 juniper berries

- Lightly dust the pork chops with flour. Sprinkle with salt and pepper.
- In a large, skillet, melt shortening. Brown pork chops over medium-high heat for about 1 minute on each side.
- Add sauerkraut and juniper berries. Distribute evenly in skillet and cook over medium heat for 25 to30 minutes.
- Serve with potato dish of your choice. A bit of applesauce is also a nice addition.
- Serves 6.

Braised Pork Chops with Sauerkraut # 2

4 thickly sliced bacon strips
2 - 2 ½ pounds sauerkraut
1 large onion, sliced
Salt
Freshly ground black pepper
2 tablespoons butter
4 pork loin chops, cut 1-inch thick
1 clove garlic, finely chopped
Beer

- Place bacon strips evenly in the bottom of a heavy braising pan.
- Rinse sauerkraut with cold water and squeeze out liquid. Put half of the sauerkraut into the pan, spreading evenly to cover bacon. Sprinkle with 1 teaspoon black pepper.

- Melt the butter in a skillet and brown pork chops on both sides over medium-high heat, 1 minute on each. When browned, arrange pork chops on top of the sauerkraut. Season to taste with salt and pepper and sprinkle with garlic.
- Add remaining sauerkraut, sprinkle with a bit more pepper, and then add enough beer to cover, about 2 cups.
- Bring to a boil, then reduce heat and simmer, covered, for 1 hour.
- Serve with potatoes of your choice, applesauce, or sautéed apple rings (remove cores from unpeeled apples and cut in ½-inch thick slices, then sauté in unsalted butter or vegetable oil). Also serve mugs of your favorite cold beer. An excellent meal!
- Serves 4.

Crockpot Sweet and Sour Kraut with Pork Chops

2 large potatoes, peeled and sliced
½ cup chopped onion
1 ½ cups sauerkraut, drained
1 tablespoon brown sugar
1 ½ cups unsweetened pineapple juice
3 average-sized pork chops, trimmed
Black pepper to taste

- Put potatoes into crockpot; top with chopped onion. Combine sauerkraut with brown sugar and pineapple juice; spoon approximately half of it over potatoes and sprinkle with a dash of pepper. Place pork chops on top of sauerkraut layer. Spoon remaining sauerkraut mixture on top; sprinkle with a dash of pepper.
- Cover and cook on high heat for 2 to 2 ½ hours or on low heat for 4 to 5 hours, until potatoes and pork chops are cooked.
- Serve with rye bread and baked apples. Serves 3.

Pork Roast Vienna

4 tablespoons cooking oil
3 ½ cups sauerkraut, drained
2 tart apples, chopped
½ cup raisins
½ to 1 cup bread crumbs
½ teaspoon celery seeds
Pork shoulder

- Using a large skillet, sauté sauerkraut, apples, raisins, breadcrumbs, and celery seeds.
- Remove bone from pork shoulder and fill cavity with sauerkraut stuffing. Sew or skewer together. Put into a shallow roasting pan and roast, uncovered, at 350 degrees Fahrenheit. Roast 30 minutes per pound, or until done. Add a small amount of water to pan if bottom gets too dry.

Danish Pork Roast and Sauerkraut in Beer

4 cups sauerkraut
1 medium onion, chopped
2 cloves garlic, chopped
1 teaspoon black pepper
3 - 4 cups beer
2 strips bacon (optional)
2 ½ - 3 pounds pork roast

- Put the sauerkraut, onion, garlic, pepper, and beer into a small pot; bring to a boil, then reduce heat and simmer, uncovered, over low heat for about 1 hour, until beer has been cooked out and absorbed by the sauerkraut.
- Brown the pork roast on all sides. Put roast into a baking or roasting pan and place the sauerkraut around the roast in a baking or roasting pan. (If smoky flavor is preferred in sauerkraut, place 2 strips bacon on the bottom of pan). Cook in a preheated 325 degree Fahrenheit oven for 1 to 1 ½ hours, until very tender.

- Serve with boiled potatoes, grated fresh horseradish, and beet and apple salad.
- Serves 4 to 5.

Krauted Pork Kabobs

½ cup sauerkraut juice
½ cup olive oil
¼ cup apple cider vinegar
¼ cup soy sauce
2 teaspoons Worcestershire sauce
2 small onions, thinly sliced
3 cloves garlic, crushed
1 teaspoon coarsely ground black pepper
1 teaspoon dry mustard
1 ½ pounds pork butt or pork shoulder, cut in 1 - 1 ½-inch cubes

- In a large bowl, first combine all ingredients except pork, mix well, then add pork cubes to marinade and toss to coat thoroughly. Cover and marinate for 4 to 6 hours in refrigerator.
- Remove meat from marinade, put on skewers, and grill on high heat for one minute. Reduce heat to medium and cook 10 to 12 minutes, turning once. Serve with heated sauerkraut and grilled vegetables.
- Serves 6 to 8.

Pigs' Knuckles with Sauerkraut

4 small pigs' knuckles (you can also use smoked ham hocks)
2 onions, chopped
2 cloves garlic, finely chopped
2 small Granny Smith apples, peeled, cored, and finely chopped
2 tablespoons lard or cooking oil
2 pounds sauerkraut
2 bay leaves
¼ teaspoon caraway seeds (optional)
1/8 teaspoon black pepper (optional)
1 cup dry white wine
1 cup beef stock

- Wash the pigs' knuckles and drain them thoroughly. Melt the lard in a large enamel casserole. Add the onions, garlic, and apples and sauté for about 5 minutes.
- Add the sauerkraut, bay leaves, white wine, and beef stock. Mix well.
- Press the pigs' knuckles down into the sauerkraut and cook, covered, over low heat for 1 hour, or until the meat is tender.
- Serve with boiled potatoes and a little mustard or horseradish.
- Serves 4.

Pork Hocks with Sauerkraut

2 ½ - 3 pounds pork hocks (or pork shoulder butt half, with bone)
8 to 9 cups water
1 medium onion, chopped
2 cloves garlic, chopped
1 tablespoon salt
1 tablespoon mixed pickling spice
4 cups sauerkraut, rinsed and drained
1 - 2 tablespoons apple sauce (optional)

- Scrub pork hocks thoroughly. Place them in a large saucepan or pot and add water to cover. Add onion, garlic, salt, and pickling spice. Bring to a boil, then reduce heat; cover tightly and simmer 1 ½ to 2 hours, or until meat is tender. Skim off fat. Strain cooking liquid. Return 1 cup liquid to saucepan or pot. Return hocks to pot and arrange sauerkraut around hocks. Add applesauce if preferred. Simmer 10 to 15 minutes, or until cabbage is tender. Drain. Serve hocks or pork shoulder butt surrounded by sauerkraut on a hot platter. Serve with potatoes.
- Serves 4 to 5.

Sauerkraut with Smoked Pork and Perogies

2 cups sauerkraut
1 tablespoon oil
1 2-pound bag frozen perogies (potato or potato with cheese)
1 pound smoked pork chunks, with a bit of fat
¼ teaspoon dill seed
¼ teaspoon black pepper

- Grease the bottom of a small roasting pan with oil; spread half of the sauerkraut evenly in pan.
- Arrange perogies and smoked pork evenly on top of sauerkraut, sprinkle with dill seed and pepper; spread remaining sauerkraut on top.
- Cover and bake in a 350-degree Fahrenheit oven for 45 to 50 minutes.
- Serve with vegetable salad of your choice.
- Serves 4 to 5.

Sideribs and Sauerkraut

3 pounds pork sideribs (or spareribs)
5 to 6 cups sauerkraut
1 10-ounce can beef broth
2 teaspoons paprika
½ teaspoon caraway seeds
½ teaspoon black pepper
2 to 4 tablespoons apple sauce or ½ cup peeled and diced sweet apple (optional)

- Thoroughly rinse the sauerkraut, then mix in the beef broth, paprika, caraway seeds, and black pepper. Place half of the sauerkraut mixture at the bottom of a large casserole dish or roasting pan. Arrange sideribs over sauerkraut, then top ribs with remaining sauerkraut. Cover and cook in the oven at 350 degrees Fahrenheit for 1 ¼ to 1 ½ hours, until ribs are tender. While cooking, baste ribs with the liquid two or three times, adding a bit of water if sauerkraut gets too dry. Add applesauce or apple in the last 30 minutes of cooking.
- Serve with dark rye bread or boiled potatoes and a glass of your favorite beer.
- Serves 4 to 5.

Spareribs and Sauerkraut

1 tablespoon lard or butter
4 to 5 cups sauerkraut, drained
3 tart apples, peeled, cored, and thinly sliced
1 medium onion, sliced
2 bay leaves
1 teaspoon salt
½ teaspoon freshly ground pepper
1 cup dry white wine
4 pounds spareribs, with excess fat trimmed off

- Grease the bottom of a large casserole dish with lard or butter. Spread sauerkraut evenly over the bottom. Cover with the apples, onion rings, bay leaves, salt, and pepper. Drizzle the wine over and lay the spareribs on top. Cover snugly with foil and bake for 1 hour. Remove foil and bake another 20 minutes.
- Serves 4 to 5.

Spareribs and Sauerkraut

2 pounds spareribs
6 large potatoes
3 cups sauerkraut, rinsed and drained
1 pound smoked farmer sausage, sliced
2 - 2 ½ cups hot water

- Arrange spareribs in a jellyroll pan and bake at 325 degrees Fahrenheit for 30 minutes, until spareribs are browned. Drain fat.
- Peel and slice potatoes.
- Lightly grease a large casserole dish and place ingredients in layers in the following order: potatoes, sauerkraut, spareribs, and sausage. Repeat layers ending with a mixture of sauerkraut and potato slices. Pour hot water over and cover tightly.

- Bake at 350 degrees Fahrenheit for 1 to 1 ½ hours, until tender. While baking, check moisture and add more hot water if casserole gets too dry.

Pork Riblets with Sauerkraut and Potatoes

3 pounds pork riblets
3 cups sauerkraut, with juice
1 pound tomatoes, quartered
¼ teaspoon black pepper
½ cup mushroom and onion soup, from can
¼ teaspoon caraway seeds
¼ teaspoon paprika
3 - 4 large potatoes, peeled and quartered

- Put all ingredients into a large roasting pan and toss to mix, coating the riblets well.
- Put in 350 degree Fahrenheit oven and cook for 30 minutes.
- Add potatoes; spoon sauerkraut and liquid over them. Cook for another 30 minutes, until potatoes are soft.
- Serves 4.

Sauerkraut with Spareribs and Dumplings

1 ½ pounds spareribs
1 quart sauerkraut
½ tablespoon sugar or 1 tablespoon raisins
Dumplings
1 ½ cups flour
½ teaspoon salt
1 tablespoon baking powder
1 egg
1 tablespoon melted butter
about 1/3 cup milk

- Place spareribs into a pot and add cold water to cover. With lid askew, cook until nearly tender. Add sauerkraut. If using raisins, add them at this time. Continue cooking for 30 minutes. Add sugar if you wish.
- Combine dry ingredients.
- Beat egg and butter together, then mix well with flour. Add milk to make a batter stiff enough to drop from a spoon. Drop into boiling sauerkraut and meat.
- Cover tightly and cook 10 to 2 minutes. Serves 6 to 7.

Spareribs and Sauerkraut in Crockpot

4 cups sauerkraut, rinsed and drained
2 tablespoons flour
1 cup dry white wine
2 pounds country-style beef spareribs (can also use pork chops)
1 apple, peeled and sliced (optional)
Pepper to taste

- Put sauerkraut in crockpot. Add 2 tablespoons flour and 1 cup wine; mix well.
- Brown spareribs in a large skillet. Arrange ribs on top of the sauerkraut in crockpot. Season with pepper. Cook on low heat for 6 -10 hours, until spareribs are tender. Serves 4.

Pork Balls and Sauerkraut

1 ½ pounds ground pork
1 medium-large onion, finely chopped
¾ cup minute rice, uncooked
2 medium eggs
1 teaspoon salt
½ teaspoon ground black pepper
5 cups sauerkraut, with juice
¼ teaspoon caraway seeds (optional)
1 teaspoon cooking oil

- Combine pork, onion, rice, eggs, salt, and pepper. Mix well, then form balls the size of a golf ball.
- Add caraway seeds to sauerkraut, if preferred, and mix well. Grease the bottom of a large pot with oil and evenly arrange half of the sauerkraut and some juice at the bottom.
- Arrange the pork balls on top of the sauerkraut, and then cover these with the remaining sauerkraut and juice. Cover pot, and simmer over low heat for about 1 to 1 ¼ hours, until pork is cooked. Serve with mashed potatoes. Serves 6 to 8.

Beef Brisket with Sauerkraut

6 pounds beef brisket
1 tablespoon salt
2 teaspoons black pepper
4 cups sauerkraut, rinsed and drained
½ - 1 cup apple cider vinegar
3 tablespoon brown sugar
1 uncooked potato, grated

- Put beef brisket in a large stewing pot and add hot water to cover. Add salt and pepper and simmer 1 to 1½ hours. Add sauerkraut, vinegar, and brown sugar.
- Cook about 1 hour longer or until meat is tender. Add potatoes and cook 10 minutes longer.
- Serves 8.

Beef Brisket with Sauerkraut and Applesauce

1 19-ounce can tomatoes, or 1 pound fresh tomatoes, cut
2 cups sauerkraut
1 cup sweet applesauce
2 ½ tablespoons brown sugar
3 pounds beef brisket

- Cut undrained tomatoes, sauerkraut, applesauce, and brown sugar into a large pot and stir to mix. Bring to a quick boil. Lower heat and add brisket.
- Cover and simmer for 3 hours, until meat is tender, intermittently spooning sauce over brisket. Add a bit of water if necessary.
- Remove brisket from pot and place on a serving platter.
- With a flat spoon, scoop up excess fat from pot. Taste sauce and add salt to taste and more brown sugar if you wish. If you prefer the sauce to be thicker, add some cornstarch (mixed with a small amount of cold first water to avoid lumps) and cook till thickened.

- For best serving, prepare brisket ahead of time. Let cool completely, slice meat, cover with sauce, and refrigerate till needed. Reheat slowly and serve slices of meat and sauce. Serve with potatoes or thick noodles, some vegetable, and salad. Excellent.
- Serves 6.

Choucroute Garni
(Alsatian Cured Meats with Sauerkraut)

1 ½ pounds fresh corned beef
1 pound pastrami
3 pounds sauerkraut
2 tablespoons schmoltz (melted chicken or goose fat), or use vegetable oil
1 cup onions, chopped
2 cloves garlic, crushed
2 ½ cups dry white wine
5 juniper berries, 4 peppercorns, 1 clove, and 1 bay leaf (tied in a cheesecloth)
½ pound highly seasoned sausages such as knockwurst or kielbasa
5 all-beef wieners
10 small new potatoes

- Partially cook the corned beef and pastrami in water to cover for about 45 minutes. Drain.
- Rinse the sauerkraut with cold water. Drain and squeeze to remove the liquid.
- Using a heavy pot, heat the schmoltz over medium heat. Add onions and sauté until soft. Add the sauerkraut, wine, garlic, and spices; heat to a low boil.
- Arrange the corned beef and pastrami on top of the sauerkraut, cover the pot, and simmer over low heat for 2 hours.
- Add the sausages and continue cooking over low heat for 1 hour. Add the wieners and new potatoes about 15 minutes before serving.
- To serve, place the sauerkraut on a serving plate; arrange the meats, sausages, wieners, and potatoes on top.
- Serves 5.

Sausages with Sauerkraut

This is a classic recipe. I've made it a few times, but never exactly the same for it depended on what kind of sausages that were available to me. Although you can use a combination of all the sausages listed, two types would be sufficient. You may use one whole large kielbasa, cotechino, or garlic sausage and 9 to 12 small sausages listed in the recipe.

2 pounds sauerkraut, rinsed and well drained
10 strips of bacon or 4 strips of thickly sliced salt pork
1 medium onion, peeled and sliced
2 – 2 ½ cups beef or chicken broth
One 1 to 1 ½ pounds kielbasa, cotechino, or garlic sausage
12 green onions, chopped
Dry red wine
3 - 4 each of bratwurst, weiswurst, and knockwurst, or 9 -12 of any one of these
2 tablespoons butter

- Place the bacon or salt pork evenly at the bottom of a large saucepan. Add the sauerkraut and the onion. Add beef or chicken broth to cover. Bring to a boil, cover, and simmer for 35 to 40 minutes.
- While sauerkraut is simmering, place the large sausages and green onions in a deep skillet; add enough red wine to barely cover. Bring to a boil; reduce heat and poach for 30 to 35 minutes, making sure to turn the sausages several times.
- At the same time, place the small sausages in another skillet and add water to barely cover. Bring to a boil; reduce heat, and poach sausages for 8 to10 minutes. Remove sausages and drain skillet. Return skillet to burner, add the butter, and sauté the small sausages over medium heat until lightly browned.
- Place sauerkraut onto a large serving plate or shallow serving dish. Cut the small sausages into halves and thickly slice the large one and place onto plate. Serve with boiled potatoes and a bit of mustard. Serve with a glass of dry white wine or cold beer. Excellent.
- Serves 8.

Farmer Sausages with Sauerkraut

1 pound farmer sausages (non-garlic)
3 - 4 cups sauerkraut
½ cup onion
2 tablespoons butter
2 cloves garlic, grated (optional)
½ teaspoon freshly ground black pepper

- Cut sausages in thin slices.
- Drain sauerkraut.
- Sauté onion in butter until onion is soft.
- Put all ingredients into a casserole, mixing well, and bake for 350 degrees Fahrenheit for 45 minutes.
- Serve with potatoes or noodles.
- Serves 5.

Beer Braised Sauerkraut with Sausages

1 ½ cups sauerkraut
6 strips smoked bacon, cut crosswise in ½-inch pieces
3 medium onions, thinly sliced
3 medium carrots, cut crosswise in ¼-inch pieces
2 cups beer
1 10-ounce can condensed chicken broth
4 bay leaves
¼ teaspoon paprika
1 teaspoon salt
¼ teaspoon black pepper
1 ¾ pounds smoked fresh sausages (frankfurters, bauernwurst, or bratwurst)

- Rinse and drain sauerkraut.
- In a large skillet, cook bacon and onions for 10 minutes over medium heat, until onions are golden brown. Remove from skillet, reserving 1 tablespoon bacon grease in skillet.
- Put sauerkraut, bacon and onions, carrots, beer, chicken broth, bay leaves, paprika, salt, and pepper into a large flameproof roasting pan or Dutch oven. Cook over medium, uncovered, for about an hour, until liquid has been cooked out.
- Cook sausages in the skillet for 15 to 20 minutes, until cooked through. Drain grease from sausages before serving.
- Serve sauerkraut with the sausages, along with your favorite beer.
- Serves 5.

Sauerkraut and Smoked Sausage in Crockpot

1 tablespoon olive oil
8 juniper berries, crushed
1 pound smoked sausage
2 pounds sauerkraut, rinsed and drained
1 medium onion, chopped
1 medium carrot, grated
3 cloves garlic, chopped
2 ½ tablespoons brown sugar
1 ½ teaspoons caraway seeds
½ teaspoon dill weed
1 cup dry white wine or beer

- Grease the bottom of crockpot with oil. Drop juniper berries into pot.
- Cut sausage at an angle in 2-inch lengths and arrange in the bottom of crockpot.
- In a bowl, toss and mix the sauerkraut, onion, garlic, carrot, brown sugar, caraway seeds, and dill weed. Add mixture to crockpot on top of the sausage. Pour the white wine over and place the lid on the crockpot. Cook on the high setting for 1 hour, then reduce heat to lower setting and cook another 4 to5 hours. Do not remove the lid from the crockpot during cooking.
- Serve with mashed potatoes, dark rye bread, and spiced apples or applesauce.

Sauerkraut Quiche

1 9-inch deep-dish pie shell
1 6 ½-ounce can tuna or chicken
½ cup onion, chopped
1 cup sauerkraut, well-drained
1 10-ounce can evaporated milk
2 medium eggs
¼ teaspoon garlic powder
½ teaspoon basil
¼ teaspoon ground cinnamon (optional)
½ teaspoon tarragon
2 teaspoons parsley
1 cup Swiss cheese, coarsely grated

- Spread tuna or chicken evenly in pie shell, and then onions and sauerkraut.
- Combine milk, eggs, and spices; beat to mix well. Pour over sauerkraut. Top with Swiss cheese.
- Bake in a 350 degree Fahrenheit oven for 45 minutes, until golden brown and a knife inserted in the center comes out clean.
- Serves 4 to 5.

Sauerkraut Sausage Quiche

2 cups sauerkraut, rinsed, drained, and chopped
½ cup finely chopped onion
2 teaspoons oil
1 cup chopped polish or other similar sausage
¼ cup finely chopped fresh parsley
½ teaspoon caraway seeds, crushed
3 eggs, beaten
1 cup light cream
2 tablespoons mayonnaise
1 teaspoon paprika
1 teaspoon cornstarch
1 ½ cups shredded Swiss cheese
1 9-inch deep dish pie crust

- Preheat the oven to 350 degrees Fahrenheit.
- Using a skillet, sauté sauerkraut and onions in 2 teaspoons oil for 5 minutes. Reduce heat to medium-low and add chopped sausages, parsley, and caraway seeds; cook for about 10 minutes, stirring once of twice. Take off heat and let cool to lukewarm.
- Beat eggs; combine with cream, mayonnaise, paprika, and cornstarch. Mix well.
- Combine sauerkraut and sausages mixture with egg and cream mixture. Pour into pie shell. Top evenly with shredded cheese.
- Bake at 350 degrees Fahrenheit for 25 to 30, minutes, until a knife inserted in the center comes out clean.
- Let cool slightly and serve. Serves 4 to 5.

Sauerkraut and Bacon Omelet

8 slices bacon
1 cup sauerkraut
4 eggs
¼ cup milk
1 tablespoon chives
1/8 teaspoon dill seeds
1/8 teaspoon black pepper
oil (olive, grapeseed, corn, or sunflower)
Paprika (optional)

- Place bacon in a non-stick skillet and fry until quite crisp, but not burnt. You may need to drain the fat before bacon is crisp enough. When done, drain the bacon well. The best way to mop up the grease is to place a non-bleached napkin on a plate and lay bacon on top, folding napkin over to soak up the grease on top as well. Break bacon strips into one-inch pieces and set aside. Clean the skillet or at least remove all the grease.
- Put sauerkraut in a sieve and run hot water over it for a few seconds, then squeeze out excess juice. You could skip that part, but I find that if you don't rinse the sauerkraut it tends to overpower the flavor of the other ingredients.
- Beat eggs and milk together in a bowl. Mix in chives, dill seeds, and pepper. Add bacon and sauerkraut; stir to mix slightly.
- Heat the skillet to medium heat, and then pour in omelet mixture. Cook until eggs are done. Don't overcook, as that will make the omelet too dry. Dust lightly with paprika if you wish.
- Serve with common breakfast fare such as toast, hashbrowns, a bit of fruit, and your favorite morning beverage.
- Serves 2.

Sauerkraut Pizza # 1

½ pound pepperoni sausages, sliced
1 small onion, chopped
1 ½ cups sauerkraut, rinsed and drained
1 7 ½-can tomato sauce
½ teaspoon basil leaves
1 green pepper, cut into thin strips
10 ounces mozzarella cheese, shredded
1 12-ounce tube refrigerated pizza dough
Cooking oil
Parmesan cheese

- In a skillet, brown sausage and onion; drain drippings. Stir in sauerkraut, tomato sauce, and basil; heat through.
- Preheat oven to 450 degrees Fahrenheit. While oven is heating, prepare green peppers and cheese.
- Prepare pizza dough according to directions on the can. Pat out the dough in a lightly greased 9x13-inch jellyroll baking pan. Brush dough with oil. Spread sauerkraut and sausage mixture over pizza dough. Top with green pepper and cheeses.
- Bake 15 to 20 minutes.
- Makes 1 9x13-inch pizza.

Sauerkraut Pizza # 2

1 12-ounce tube refrigerated pizza dough
1 pound raw pork sausages, sliced
1 cup chopped onion
1 ½ teaspoons fennel seed, cracked
1 teaspoon dried oregano
1 teaspoon dried basil
2 cloves garlic, minced
2 cups shredded mozzarella cheese
1 14-ounce can pizza sauce
1 14-ounce can diced tomatoes
2 cups sauerkraut, drained
¼ cup Parmesan cheese

- Preheat oven to 450 degrees Fahrenheit.
- Roll out pizza dough according to package instructions. Press into a 14-inch round pizza pan or a 9x13-inch jellyroll baking pan. Bake in pre-heated oven for 4 minutes; remove from oven and set aside.
- In a large skillet, cook sausage, onion, 1 teaspoon of fennel seed, oregano, basil, and garlic until the onion is tender. Drain.
- Sprinkle crust with ½ cup mozzarella cheese. Spread with pizza sauce, sausage mixture, tomatoes, sauerkraut, and the remaining fennel seed. Top with remaining mozzarella cheese and the Parmesan cheese.
- Bake at 450 degrees Fahrenheit for 15 to 20 minutes, or until golden brown and bubbly. Let stand for 5 minutes before cutting.
- Serves 6.

Sauerkraut Pizza # 3

1 12-ounce tube refrigerated pizza dough
¾ pound spicy pork sausage meat
1 cup sauerkraut, rinsed and drained
1 teaspoon Cajun seasoning
¼ teaspoon caraway seeds, crushed
2 tablespoons sour cream
1 7 ½-ounce can tomato sauce
1 medium tomato, thinly sliced
1 cup thinly sliced green bell pepper
½ pound mozzarella cheese, shredded

- In a skillet, brown sausage meat, breaking up lumps with a fork. Drain fat, reserving 1 tablespoon drippings; set meat aside.
- Put sauerkraut into skillet. Add Cajun seasoning and caraway seeds. Sauté for 5 minutes. Remove from heat and stir in sour cream.
- Preheat oven to 450 degrees Fahrenheit. While oven is heating, prepare tomato, pepper, and cheese. Roll out pizza dough according to package instructions. Press into a lightly greased 14-inch round pizza pan or a 9x13-inch jellyroll baking pan.
- Add tomato sauce to dough and spread evenly. Add browned sausage meat. Top with sauerkraut, tomato slices, green pepper, and cheese in the order give. Place in oven and bake for 15 to 20 minutes, until pizza is cooked through and cheese is melted and lightly browned. Remove from oven and let stand for 5 minutes before cutting.
- Serves 4.

Sauerkraut and Pasta Primavera

1/3 cup olive oil
3 cloves garlic, minced
1 to 2 teaspoons dried dill weed
3 tablespoons red wine vinegar or apple cider vinegar
Salt and pepper
2 cups frozen peas, thawed
¼ cup chopped pickled hot peppers
2 cups sauerkraut, rinsed and liquid squeezed out
2 cups fresh mushrooms, sliced
2 cups frozen tiny cooked shrimp, thawed
1 pound fettuccine, rotini or rotelle pasta
Parmesan cheese

- Combine oil, garlic, dill, vinegar, salt, and pepper; let sit for 30 minutes.
- Toss peas, hot peppers, sauerkraut, mushrooms, and shrimp in oil mixture.
- Cook pasta until soft; drain.
- While pasta is cooking, heat oil and vegetable mixture in skillet until heated through. Add to drained pasta and toss to mix. Sprinkle with Parmesan cheese.
- Serve hot or cold. Serves 4 to 5.

Meatballs with Sauerkraut and Cranberry Sauce

2 pounds lean ground beef
2 envelopes dry onion soup mix
1 cup dry bread crumbs soaked in 1 cup water
3 medium eggs
3 cups sauerkraut, drained
1 14-ounce can whole berry cranberry sauce
¼ cup finely chopped pickled hot peppers (or use fresh)
½ cup brown sugar, firm
½ cup water

- In a large mixing bowl, combine ground beef, onion soup mix, soaked breadcrumbs, and eggs. Mix well and form into 1 ½-inch meatballs. Place meatballs in a 13x9x2-inch casserole.
- In a large skillet, combine sauerkraut, cranberry sauce, chopped peppers, brown sugar, and water. Bring to a boil, then simmer for 5 minutes.
- Evenly pour sauerkraut mixture over meatballs. Bake, uncovered, at 350 degrees Fahrenheit for 45 to 60 minutes, until meatballs are cooked through.
- Serves 6 to 8.

Sauerkraut Lasagna
(German)

12 lasagna noodles
1 10-ounce can cream of mushroom soup
1 10-ounce can cream of chicken soup
2 ¼ cups milk
1 pound kielbasa
2 ½ cups sauerkraut, drained
8 ounces mozzarella cheese, shredded

- Put pasta in lightly salted water and bring to a boil. Boil over medium high heat for two minutes, then reduce heat to medium low and cook for about 8 minutes, until noodles are soft. Remove from water and drain.
- Using a blender or whisk, blend mushroom soup, cream of chicken soup, and milk until smooth.
- Cut sausage in half lengthwise and slice thinly.
- Lightly grease a 9x13-inch casserole dish. Pour in a layer of soup mixture (1 cup). Arrange 4 noodles over top, then half the sauerkraut, followed with half the sausage and a third of the cheese. Repeat. Top with remaining 4 noodles and remaining soup mixture.
- Cover with foil and bake in a preheated 350 degree Fahrenheit oven for 30 minutes, then uncover and bake 15 minutes more. Sprinkle with remaining cheese when still hot.
- Makes 1 9x13-inch lasagna.

Bierocks
(Bread rolls with zesty meat and sauerkraut stuffing)

Filling
1 ½ pounds ground beef
1 cup shredded cabbage
1 envelope onion soup mix
1 ½ cups sauerkraut
¾ teaspoon salt
½ teaspoon pepper
¾ cup water

Dough
¾ cup warm water
1 package of active dry yeast
1 teaspoon sugar
1 cup mashed potatoes
1 egg
1/3 cup salad oil
3 to 3 ¼ cups all-purpose flour

Eggwash
1 egg, beaten
1 tablespoon water

- In a large skillet, brown meat; drain off the fat. Stir in remaining filling ingredients. Cook, uncovered for 10 to 15 minutes until the liquid is absorbed; stir occasionally as needed.
- In a large mixing bowl, combine water, yeast, and sugar. Let stand for 5 to 7 minutes until foamy. Add mashed potatoes, 1 egg, and oil; beat with a whisk until well blended. Add flour slowly while beating, then kneading until a stiff dough forms. Place dough onto a floured surface and knead until smooth, 2 to 3 minutes. Divide the dough in twelve equal parts. Roll out each in 6 to 7-inch circles. Spoon about ¾ cup of the hamburger mixture in the center of each circle. Brush the edges with a little water, then fold over the circles to form a half-circle shape. With the tines of a fork, gently press the dough edges together to seal them. Use a table knife to trim the sealed edges so that they resemble a half moon.

Place on a greased cookie sheet. Repeat with the remaining dough and filling. Cover and let rise for about 20 minutes.

- Pre-heat the oven to 350 degrees Fahrenheit. In a small bowl combine egg and water. Brush the tops of the turnovers with the egg mixture. Bake for 15 to 20 minutes or until golden brown. Serve hot as part of a meal or cold as a quick snack. Excellent for taking on hiking trips and other outdoor activities.
- Makes 12 turnovers.

Kraut Stuffed Green Peppers

4 - 6 green peppers (depending on size)
3 tablespoons chopped onion
½ pound ground beef, chopped corned beef, or diced polish sausages
2 tablespoons butter
2 ½ cups sauerkraut
Dash of paprika
¼ teaspoon celery seeds or Worcestershire sauce
1 cup buttered breadcrumbs

- Cut peppers in half (lengthwise), remove seeds, and parboil them for 10 minutes.
- Sauté onion and beef in butter. Add sauerkraut, paprika, and celery seeds or Worcestershire sauce. Cook for about 15 minutes.
- Stuff peppers with sauerkraut mixture and top with buttered breadcrumbs. Place peppers on skillet and heat through. Serve with sauce made of celery or onion soup.

Bavarian Beef Patties with Sauerkraut

1 ½ pounds ground beef
½ cup applesauce
1/3 cup dried breadcrumbs
1 small onion, chopped fine
1 large egg
1 teaspoon salt
½ teaspoon allspice
2 cups sauerkraut, drained

- Mix all the ingredients except the sauerkraut.
- Press mixture into six ¾-inch thick patties.
- Brown the patties in a large skillet over medium heat, turning once. Drain off excess fat. If you use extra lean beef, there'll hardly be any fat. In fact, you may need to oil the skillet lightly.
- Spoon the sauerkraut onto the patties and simmer for about 15 minutes, turning once. Serve patties and sauerkraut along with vegetable dish of your choice. You may also serve the patties and sauerkraut on white or whole-wheat buns. They are excellent.
- Serves 6.

Chicken in the Pot

3 cups chicken broth
2 ½ pounds chicken pieces
½ cup diced carrots
1 medium onion, sliced
2 cloves garlic, chopped
2 cups sauerkraut, drained
2 bay leaves
4 juniper berries
1 ¾ cups peeled and chopped tomatoes
½ teaspoon salt
½ teasppon black pepper

- In a large heavy pot bring chicken broth to a boil. Add chicken pieces; reduce heat to low and cook, uncovered, for 30 minutes.
- Add carrots, onion, sauerkraut, bay leaf, and juniper berries. Cover and simmer 30 minutes. Add tomatoes and season with salt and pepper 10 minutes before the end of cooking time. Serve with boiled potatoes.
- Serves 4.

Greek-Style Chicken with Sauerkraut

1 3 ½-pound chicken (or thighs)
1 ½ cups onions, chopped
2 cloves garlic, finely chopped
¾ cup chopped celery
3 cups sauerkraut, drained
1 14-ounce can stewed tomatoes
1 tablespoon lemon juice
¼ teaspoon grated lemon zest
¼ teaspoon cinnamon
Pepper to taste

- Using a sharp knife or cleaver, cut or chop chicken into bit-size pieces. Place in a large deep skillet set over medium-high heat. Cook, turning, until browned all over. Remove from skillet and set aside. Leave drippings from chicken in skillet. Reduce heat to medium.
- Add the onions and garlic to the skillet and cook, stirring, until the onions are tender. Add the celery, sauerkraut, tomatoes, lemon juice, lemon zest, cinnamon, and pepper. Simmer for about 40 minutes, or until the chicken is fork tender and cooked through. Serve with salad of your choice.
- Serves 4 to 6.

Sweet and Sour Fried Chicken

1 2 ½-pound chicken, cut in pieces
Cooking oil, for frying chicken
½ cup finely chopped onions
1 cup sauerkraut
¼ to 1/3 cup sauerkraut juice
¼ to ½ teaspoon Cajun seasoning, to taste
3 - 4 tablespoons honey
1/8 teaspoon black pepper

- Pour oil (about 2 inches deep) in a large heavy saucepan. Add chicken and fry over medium heat until cooked through. Remove chicken from pan and set aside.
- Put 3 tablespoons of the oil used for cooking the chicken into a large skillet and cook chopped onions over low-medium heat until soft. Add sauerkraut and juice. Cook 5 minutes, then add remaining ingredients including the fried chicken pieces. Mix well. Reduce heat to low and simmer, uncovered, stirring now and then, until most of the liquid is absorbed, about 10 to 15 minutes. During the last stage, taste-test chicken and sauerkraut; add more sauerkraut juice and honey, if desired.
- Excellent with fried potatoes or Potato Sauerkraut Casserole (check side dishes in this cookbook). Serve with a salad of your choice.
- Serves 4.

Sauerkraut and Chicken Stir Fry

2 tablespoons sherry or brandy
1 tablespoon soy sauce
2 tablespoons cornstarch
½ tablespoon finely chopped garlic
2 tablespoons vegetable oil or butter
1 boneless chicken breast (about ¾ pound), cut in bite-sized pieces
1/3 cup red pepper julienne
1/3 cup green pepper julienne
1/3 cup snow pea julienne
1/3 cup carrot julienne
3 to 4 cups sauerkraut, drained
3 green onions, chopped
½ cup cashews or almonds (or a combination of both)

- In a small bowl, mix sherry or brandy, soy sauce, cornstarch, and garlic.
- Using a large skillet, heat oil at medium temperature. Add chicken and sherry mixture. Sauté, stirring constantly, until chicken is cooked. Remove chicken and set aside. Add peppers, snow peas, and carrots to skillet and cook for 2 to 3 minutes, stirring steadily. Stir in sauerkraut and cook until heated through. Add chicken along with green onions and sauté 2 to 3 more minutes. Sprinkle with cashews or almonds. Serve immediately.
- Serves 4.

Krauted Chicken Pie

3 teaspoons cooking oil
2 cups finely chopped chicken meat
½ cup finely chopped potato
¼ cup finely chopped celery
¼ cup chopped onion
2 cloves garlic, finely chopped
¾ cup sauerkraut with 2 tablespoons juice
½ teaspoon parsley
¼ teaspoon caraway seeds
¼ teaspoon paprika (optional)
2 eggs
2 tablespoons chicken stock
Salt and black pepper to taste (about 1/8 teaspoon of each)
1 9-inch deep-dish pie shell, with top
Sour cream

- Using a small skillet, brown chicken in 1 ½ teaspoons oil. Remove from pan and set aside.
- Put potato, celery, onion, and 1 ½ teaspoons cooking oil in skillet and sauté for 5 minutes. Add garlic, sauerkraut parsley, caraway seeds, and paprika, if desired; sauté another 5 minutes. Remove from heat and let cool slightly. Beat eggs lightly; add chicken stock and season to taste with pepper and salt. If chicken stock is not available, use 1 tablespoon butter and 1 tablespoon water. Add chicken and stir to mix lightly.
- Put mixture into pie shell and add top part. Press edges with a fork and make a few slits with a knife for steam escape.
- Bake for 10 minutes at 425 degrees Fahrenheit, then reduce heat to 350 degrees Fahrenheit and continue baking for another 25 to 30 minutes. Serve with sour cream.
- Serves 4 to 5.

Kraut Chicken Parmesan

2 pounds boneless, skinless chicken breasts
2 eggs, beaten with 1 tablespoon olive oil
1 cup dry bread crumbs, crushed fine
¼ teaspoon each of oregano, sage, thyme, and basil
1/8 teaspoon cayenne pepper
2 to 3 tablespoons olive or grape-seed oil
2 7 ½-ounce cans tomato sauce
2 cups sauerkraut, rinsed and drained
¼ cup grated Parmesan cheese
1 ½ cups mozzarella cheese, shredded

- Combine breadcrumbs, herbs, and cayenne pepper. Dip chicken into eggs then roll in the breadcrumbs.
- Grease the bottom of a large casserole or a roasting pan with 2 tablespoons oil. Arrange chicken breasts in pan and bake at 400 degrees Fahrenheit until almost done. Lower oven to 350 degrees Fahrenheit.
- Pour sauce evenly on top of chicken, then cover with sauerkraut. Sprinkle with Parmesan cheese and bake until heated, 5 to 10 minutes. Top with Mozzarella cheese and bake another 5 minutes or until cheese is melted. Serve with garlic toast.
- Serves 4.

Baked Chicken Reuben

4 boneless, skinless, chicken breast halves
Salt and pepper to taste
2 ½ cups sauerkraut, drained
4 slices Swiss Cheese
1 - 1 ½ cups Thousand Island dressing

- Situate the oven rack in the middle position and preheat oven to 350 degrees Fahrenheit.
- Pat the chicken breasts dry using paper towels and place them into a lightly greased shallow baking pan. Season with salt and pepper; spoon the sauerkraut over chicken. Top each breast with a slice of Swiss cheese and pour the dressing evenly over the breasts.
- Cover the pan and bake the chicken for about 1 hour, until chicken is fork tender.
- Serve hot. Serves 4.

Crockpot Chicken Reuben

4 cups sauerkraut, rinsed and drained
1 cup Russian or Thousand Island dressing
6 whole boneless, skinless chicken breasts, halved
1 ½ tablespoons brown Dijon prepared mustard
1 teaspoon caraway seeds (optional)
½ teaspoon black pepper
½ cup beer or chicken broth
1 cup shredded Swiss cheese

- Place 2 cups of the sauerkraut in a large crockpot. Add ½ cup of the Russian dressing. Place 6 chicken breast halves on top; spread the mustard over the chicken. Top with remaining sauerkraut, chicken breasts, and dressing. Pour in beer or chicken broth.
- Cover and cook at low temperature setting for about 4 hours, until chicken is fork tender.
- Sprinkle cheese over top and cook until melted. Serve with crusty rye or French bread and potatoes. Serves 6.

Chicken Thighs with Sauerkraut

¼ pound bacon, chopped
1 medium onion, chopped
8 chicken thighs (2 pounds)
1 ½ cups chicken broth
¼ cup flour
1 teaspoon caraway seeds, crushed
4 cups sauerkraut, drained
Salt and pepper

- In a large skillet, fry bacon until almost crisp. Add onion and fry, stirring occasionally, for 3 to 5 minutes. Add chicken thighs and brown on both sides.
- Mix broth and flour; add to pan and cook for a few minutes. Stir in Sauerkraut and caraway seeds; season with salt and pepper. Reduce heat to low and simmer until chicken is cooked through, about 45 minutes. Serve with potatoes or dumplings. Serves 4.

Chicken Cooked in Sauerkraut

¼ pound butter
1 ½ pounds sauerkraut
2 cloves garlic, crushed or finely grated
1 average-sized frying chicken, cut in 8 pieces
8 small red-skinned potatoes, peeled
Sour cream

- Heat the butter over low heat in a large pot just until it's melted. Add the sauerkraut with all its juice and the garlic. Mix well. Add the chicken pieces and the potatoes; mix everything well, making sure the sauerkraut covers the chicken and potatoes.
- Cover and cook over low to medium heat for one 1 to 1 ¼ hours, stirring occasionally. Serve with the sour cream on the side, buttered rye bread, and beer.
- Serves 6 to 8.

Crockpot Chicken and Sauerkraut

1 3-pound whole chicken, washed and dried
1 cup sauerkraut, drained
1 tablespoon brown sugar
1 clove chopped garlic (optional)
Salt and pepper to taste

- Sprinkle sauerkraut with brown sugar; add garlic, if preferred, and season with salt and pepper to taste.
- Stuff chicken with sauerkraut mixture and put into a crock-pot. Add water to barely cover.
- Put lid on pot, turn heat to high and cook chicken for about 3 hours.
- Serve chicken and sauerkraut with mashed potatoes and salad.
- Serves 3 to 4.

Chicken with Sauerkraut

2 tablespoons vegetable oil
6 large chicken breast halves
1 ½ cups sliced potatoes
2 - 3 cups sauerkraut, drained
½ teaspoon caraway seeds
¼ teaspoon crushed red pepper
Sour cream

- Heat oil in a large skillet. Brown chicken on both sides, about 15 minutes. Drain fat. Add potatoes to skillet, arranging evenly. Mix sauerkraut, caraway seeds, and red pepper. Spoon over potatoes.
- Cover and cook over low heat for about 40 minutes, until chicken is done.
- Serve with sour cream. Serves 6.

Chicken Sauerkraut Bake

4 boneless, skinless chicken breast halves
2 cups sauerkraut, rinsed and drained
1 teaspoon garlic powder
1/8 teaspoon cayenne pepper
1 cup barbecue sauce
1 cup shredded Mozzarella or Swiss cheese (optional)

- Spread sauerkraut evenly on the bottom of a lightly greased 11x7-inch baking pan or casserole. Place chicken breasts on top, and sprinkle with garlic powder. Spread barbecue sauce over chicken. Cover and bake at 350 degrees Fahrenheit for 50 to 60 minutes, until chicken is done. If preferred, top with cheese in the last 10 minutes of baking.
- Serve with boiled potatoes. Serves 4.

Baked Chicken and Sauerkraut

1 3 ½-pound chicken
2 - 3 cloves garlic, finely grated
1/3 cup sweet wine
¼ cup olive or grape seed oil
1 medium-sized green bell pepper, cut in thin slivers
3 - 4 cups sauerkraut, rinsed and all juice squeezed out
½ teaspoon black pepper

- Cut chicken in eight parts; rub with garlic and sprinkle with pepper. To marinate, put the chicken, wine, and oil into a strong plastic bag, squeeze out all the air and tie tightly. Refrigerate for at least 4 hours. Arrange pieces of chicken in a casserole dish or roasting pan, with slivers of bell pepper between them. Top with enough sauerkraut to cover chicken. Pour the remaining marinade on top.
- Cover and cook in a 350-degree Fahrenheit oven for 1 to 1 ¼ hours, until chicken is cooked. Serve with baked potatoes or rice.

Chicken Meatball Kraut Skillet

2 eggs, slightly beaten
½ cup skim milk
3 cups fine bread crumbs
1 teaspoon salt
½ teaspoon black pepper
1 pound ground chicken breast
1 tablespoon cooking oil
4 cups sauerkraut, rinsed and drained
1 cup onions, chopped
¾ cup long-grain rice, cooked
2 cups water
1 14-ounce can crushed tomatoes

- Combine eggs, milk, breadcrumbs, salt, and black pepper. Add ground chicken and mix well. Shape into 12 meatballs or small patties. Heat oil in a large skillet over medium heat. Add meatballs and brown on all sides. Remove meatballs from skillet.
- In the same skillet, combine sauerkraut and onions. Stir in rice and water. Add meatballs and crushed tomatoes. Bring to a boil, then reduce heat and simmer, covered, for 30 minutes, until meatballs are cooked.
- Serves 6.

Chicken and Bratwurst with Sauerkraut

1 large Spanish onion, peeled and sliced
3 tablespoons vegetable oil
5 chicken thighs
5 smoked bratwurst
2 ½ cups chicken broth
2 pounds sauerkraut, rinsed and drained
Black pepper to taste

- Put onion and vegetable oil into a deep, wide saucepan or a Dutch oven and cook over medium-high heat for about 5 minutes, stirring occasionally, until onion is soft.
- Add chicken thighs, skin side down, and cook 5 minutes until they begin to brown. Cut the bratwurst in half lengthwise and add them to the pan along with the chicken broth.
- Add sauerkraut to pan. Cover and bring to a boil, then reduce heat and cook 30 minutes, or until the chicken is cooked.
- Serve with boiled, mashed, or baked potato and rye bread. Serves 5.

Roast Duck with Sauerkraut and Apples

1 6-pound duck
4 cups sauerkraut
4 large tart apples, such as Granny Smith
Salt and pepper
1 tablespoon paprika
3 bay leaves
¼ teaspoon caraway seed (optional)
1 cup dry white wine

- Preheat oven to 400 degrees Fahrenheit.
- Peel, core, and coarsely grate the apples. Mix with the sauerkraut; season with salt and freshly ground black pepper to taste.
- Wash and dry the duck, and prick it all over with a fork. Rub it inside and out with paprika, salt, and pepper. Stuff about ¾ of the sauerkraut and apples into the duck, or as much as will fit. Secure the cavity opening with string. Spread the remaining sauerkraut and apples, and the bay leaves and caraway seeds on the bottom of a large roasting pan; place the duck on top. Pour the wine over the duck.
- Put the duck into the oven and bake for 15 minutes at 400 degrees Fahrenheit. Reduce heat to 350 degrees and bake 1 ½ to 2 hours, until duck is tender. Baste every 15 minutes, skimming off any excess fat at the bottom of the pan, adding a bit of water if necessary. Serve with potatoes or dumplings.
- Serves 4.

Krauted Wild Duck

2 wild ducks
2 cups sauerkraut
2 cups applesauce
Salt and pepper
Paprika (optional)

- Wash ducks and dry with a paper towel. Rub inside and out with salt, pepper, and paprika. Stuff ducks with sauerkraut and place in a small roasting pan. Spoon applesauce over the ducks. Add a small amount of water to the bottom of the pan. Bake at 300 degrees until ducks are tender. Before serving ducks, remove sauerkraut and discard.

Fish with Sauerkraut

2 pounds whitefish, trout, or salmon fillets
1 cup finely chopped red onions
1/3 cup butter
3 ½ cups sauerkraut, drained
1 10-ounce can chicken broth
Black pepper
Flour
1 medium red onion, thinly sliced

- If fillets are large, cut them into serving-size pieces.
- In a large skillet, sauté 1 cup chopped onion in 2 tablespoons butter until clear. Add sauerkraut and chicken broth. Simmer, uncovered for about 35 minutes. Remove from pan and drain.
- Sprinkle fillets lightly with pepper, then dust with flour. Melt remaining butter in skillet and cook fillets 3 to 4 minutes on each side or until fish is opaque and flakes easily. Remove from pan and arrange on a serving plate, keeping it warm.
- Sauté onion rings. Spread sauerkraut over fillets and garnish with the sautéed onion rings.
- Serves 6.

Baked Fish Fillets with Sauerkraut

8 small or 4 medium-sized salmon or trout fillets (1 ¼ - 1 ½ pounds)
8 tablespoons mayonnaise
1 cup finely chopped onion
1 cup sauerkraut
1 cup diced tomatoes
1 cup bread crumbs
4 tablespoons butter
4 12-inch squares of foil

- Place each fillet in the center of a foil square. On top of each fillet place 2 tablespoons mayonnaise followed by ¼ cup onions, ¼ cup sauerkraut and ¼ cup tomatoes. Finish off with the breadcrumbs and a tablespoon of butter. Fold the sides of the foil over the middle and roll the ends up to seal.
- Place the pouches on a cookie-sheet and place in a pre-heated 350 degrees Fahrenheit oven for about 10 minutes, then turn over and continue to bake for another 10 more minutes.
- Serves 4.

Baked Fish with Sauerkraut

2 ½ pounds Northern Pike, Trout, or Whitefish fillets
Salt and pepper to taste
3 tablespoons flour
2 eggs, beaten
¼ cup fine breadcrumbs
5 tablespoons butter or cooking oil
5 cups sauerkraut, rinsed and juices squeezed out
1 cup sour cream
Grated Swiss cheese

- Salt and pepper the fish fillets, dredge with flour, dip into eggs, and sprinkle with breadcrumbs. Sauté both sides in 2 tablespoons butter or oil. In a saucepan, melt 2 tablespoons butter; add sauerkraut and cook, covered, for about 30 minutes until sauerkraut is tender. Add a bit of water if sauerkraut gets sticky.
- Preheat oven to 375 degrees Fahrenheit.
- Grease a casserole with remaining butter or oil, and layer sauerkraut and fish fillets alternately, starting with sauerkraut. Place small dollops of sour cream on each layer of fish, and sprinkle some cheese on each layer of sauerkraut. Bake about 30 minutes at 375 degrees Fahrenheit. Serve with herbed, sautéed potatoes.
- Serves 4.

Cabbage Rolls Stuffed with Sauerkraut
(Ukrainian)

10 to 15 cabbage leaves, depending on size
2 tablespoons butter
1 cup chopped green peppers
½ cup chopped onions
½ cup chopped celery
4 cups sauerkraut, drained
Salt and pepper to taste
2 cups uncooked chopped spicy sausages
4 tablespoons butter
2 7 ½-ounce cans tomato sauce

- Cook cabbage leaves in boiling salted water until soft enough so the leaves will fold nicely when assembling cabbage rolls. Drain. Cut leaves in half, along the spine. Fresh leaves sometimes break when you peel them off the head, so you may need to steam the entire head before removing the leaves. You may also use sour cabbage leaves, cut from a sour head. In this case, you will likely not need to cook or steam the leaves. They will be flexible enough to roll and fold as is.
- Using a large skillet, sauté green peppers and onions and in butter for 2 minutes; add sauerkraut and celery. Season to taste with pepper and salt. Stir and cook for 5 to 10 minutes. Add a small amount of water or soup stock if the mixture gets too dry. Remove sauerkraut mixture from skillet and set aside.
- Brown sausage meat in the skillet, then add sauerkraut mixture; mix well.
- Place 2 or more tablespoons of filling on each leaf, depending on the size of the leaves. Roll up leaves and fold ends; place folded ends down in greased casserole or roasting pan. Dot with 4 tablespoons of butter.
- Bake at 350 degrees Fahrenheit for about 25 minutes. Add tomato sauce evenly over cabbage rolls and continue baking for 10 to 15 minutes.
- Serves with potatoes or perogies. Serves 4 to 5.

Note: You may omit the tomato sauce and instead top rolls with sour cream when serving.

Samuel's Jumbo Cabbage Rolls

½ cup buckwheat
1 pound red wine-flavored pork sausages (uncooked)
1 pound ground turkey or chicken
½ cup chopped fresh parsley
1 cup minced onions
2 cloves minced garlic (optional)
¼ teaspoon pepper
1 teaspoon salt
½ teaspoon paprika
12 large sauerkraut leaves from soured whole cabbage head
1 7 ½-ounce can tomato sauce

- Rinse buckwheat and put into a saucepan; add water to cover and cook for 10 to 15 minutes until soft, but not mushy.
- Meanwhile, remove the skins from sausages; mash in a bowl using a fork. Put sausage meat and turkey into a skillet and brown.
- Mix browned meat with parsley, onions, and seasonings.
- Place ¾ to 1 cup filling on a kraut leaf, roll up and fold ends. Place cabbage roll, with folds down, into a large lightly greased Dutch oven or roasting pan. Repeat with remaining leaves. Pour tomato sauce over rolls.
- Put Dutch oven into a 350 degree Fahrenheit oven. Cook for 45 minutes.
- Serve rolls, topped with generous amounts of sour cream.
- Makes 12 large cabbage rolls, serving 4 to 6.

Barley in Cabbage Rolls
(Hungarian)

1 medium-large head of cabbage
1 pound lean ground beef
1 cup cooked pearl or pot barley
1 onion, chopped
1 egg, slightly beaten
1 teaspoon salt
2 cloves garlic, minced
¼ teaspoon allspice
3 ½ cups sauerkraut, drained
2 7 ½-ounce cans tomato sauce
¼ cup brown sugar

- There are two ways to prepare the cabbage leaves in order to make them soft and easy to peel off the head without tearing. 1. Place cabbage in the freezer for a few days. The night before making the rolls, take it out to thaw. 2. Remove the core from the cabbage head and place the head into a pot with salted water and blanch until soft enough to peel off leaves without breaking. You will find the leaves easier to roll if you cut off the thick rib at the base of the leaf.
- Combine beef, barley, onion, egg, and seasonings; place in center of leaves; dividing evenly. Roll up; fold in the edges. In a large baking dish or roasting pan, combine sauerkraut, 1 can tomato sauce, and the brown sugar; spread evenly. Place cabbage rolls, seam side down, on sauerkraut. Pour remaining tomato sauce over cabbage rolls. Cover and bake at 350 degrees Fahrenheit for 1 hour or until done. Serve with sour cream.

Sarma
(Yugoslavian Cabbage Rolls)

1 large fresh head of cabbage (or use sour cabbage)
1 pound sauerkraut, rinsed and squeezed dry
2 tablespoons olive oil
1 cup coarsely chopped white onions
2 teaspoons chopped garlic
1 pound ground lean beef **or** ½ pound beef and ½ pound pork
¼ cup minute rice
1 teaspoon fresh lemon juice
½ teaspoon rosemary
½ teaspoon sweet paprika
½ teaspoon salt
¼ teaspoon black pepper (optional)
¼ cup dry white wine
½ cup tomato purée

- There are two ways to prepare the cabbage leaves in order to make them soft and easy to peel off the head without tearing. 1. Place cabbage in the freezer for a few days. The night before making the rolls, take it out to thaw. 2. Remove the core from the cabbage head and place the head into a pot with salted water and blanch until soft enough to peel off leaves without breaking. You will find the leaves easier to roll if you cut off the thick rib at the base of the leaf. Note: If you use leaves from a soured head, you will not need to blanche the leaves. Also, you may want to use fresh cabbage (shredded and blanched) in place of the sauerkraut. If you still insist in using sauerkraut, as I do, rinse several times and squeeze dry. The rinsing will ensure that the rolls won't be too sour.
- Heat the olive oil in a large skillet. Sauté the onions over medium heat for 2 minutes. Add the garlic and ground meat. Sauté the mixture for 3 minutes while breaking up the meat clumps. Add the rice, lemon juice, rosemary, paprika, ½ of the sauerkraut, and salt and pepper. Mix thoroughly for about 1 minute, then shut off heat and let stand until cool enough to handle.
- Place 2 to 3 rounded teaspoons of the filling mixture in the middle of each cabbage leaf. Wrap the leaf around the filling, envelope-style.

- Place a ½-inch layer of sauerkraut on the bottom of a heavy casserole or roasting pan. Arrange the rolls seam side down on top of the sauerkraut. Cover rolls with the remaining sauerkraut.
- Mix the wine and tomato purée. Pour evenly over sauerkraut layer.
- Cover casserole or roasting pan and bake at 350 degrees Fahrenheit for about 1 hour. Serve the rolls hot, along with the cooked and drained sauerkraut. Top rolls with yogurt or sour cream. Excellent served with rye or pumpernickel bread, some cold beer or fruity red wine.
- Serves 4.

Bavarian Sauerkraut Rolls

Dough
2 ½ cups flour
2 to 3 eggs
3 - 5 tablespoons cold water
Salt
Filling
5 strips medium-lean bacon, diced
2 tablespoons lard or butter
2 cups sauerkraut, drained, chopped
1 small apple, peeled and grated
Other
4 tablespoons lard
Beef stock

- Combine dough ingredients and knead into pliable noodle dough, adding more flour or water depending on the consistency. On a clean, floured surface, roll dough into thin sheets and divide into smaller rectangles. Let stand, uncovered, for a short time so the dough will start to dry out.
- Meanwhile, fry the bacon in the lard until translucent. Add sauerkraut and apple to pan. Fry, turning frequently, until sauerkraut is golden yellow. Take off heat and allow mixture to cool somewhat, then spread a thin layer of filling on each of the rectangular sheets of dough, and roll them up into little bundles about 2 inches in diameter. Cut each bundle into 1 ½ to 2-inch long pieces.
- Preheat oven to 350 degrees Fahrenheit. Heat the lard in an ovenproof ceramic casserole or small roasting pan. Arrange sauerkraut rolls in the casserole with cut sides up. Pour beef stock into casserole or pan to the depth of ½ inch. Bake until rolls have acquired a bit of a crust. While baking, add a bit more stock if necessary. Also, sprinkle the tops of the rolls with beef stock. Bake for about 20 minutes.
- Serve topped with melted butter or sour cream. Serves 4.

Sauerkraut with Hungarian Beef Goulash and Dumplings

Goulash
1 ½ pounds stewing beef
2 large onions (chopped)
4 cloves garlic (chopped fine)
¼ cup butter
2 tablespoons paprika
1/8 teaspoon dill or caraway seed
1/8 teaspoon pepper
Water
2 cups sauerkraut
Dumplings
1 pound potatoes
¾ cup flour
2 egg yolks
½ teaspoon nutmeg

- Cut beef in ½-inch pieces and brown in a skillet or saucepan. Place into a large pot with onions, garlic, butter, paprika, dill or caraway seeds, pepper, and 1 ½ cups water, or to cover ingredients. Bring to a boil, then reduce heat to low and cook for 1 hour with lid of pot askew.
- Meanwhile peel potatoes; cook or steam very soft. Mash potatoes and set aside to cool.
- After goulash has been cooking for 1 hour, rinse sauerkraut slightly and add to pot. Add 1 ½ to 2 cups water. Cook another half hour.
- Meanwhile prepare dumplings. Mix together mashed potatoes, flour, egg yolks, and nutmeg. Form dumplings the size of a walnut and put into goulash. Stir to submerge dumplings. Cook for another 15 to 20 minutes.
- Serve with red cabbage dish. To prepare: Place 5 cups chopped cabbage into a saucepan. Add ½ cup water, 2 tablespoons olive oil, and 1/8 teaspoon dill seed. Cook until cabbage is quite soft. Drain. If you prefer a slight sweet taste, add a bit of maple syrup to cabbage before serving.
- Serves 5.

Vareniki
(Ukrainian)

Dough
4 cups white flour
Salt
4 large eggs (yolks and whites separated)
2 tablespoons cooking oil
¾ -1 cup water
½ cup unsalted butter
Filling
3 slices bacon, diced
1 large onion, chopped
3 ½ cups sauerkraut, rinsed and liquid squeezed out
1 ½ tablespoons tomato paste
2 teaspoons sugar
1/3 cup chicken broth

- In a mixing bowl, blend the flour and ½ teaspoon salt. Using hands, work in the egg yolks and the oil, then add the water gradually while kneading mixture into a ball. Transfer dough to a floured surface and knead until smooth, about two minutes. Cover with a linen or cotton kitchen towel and let stand 30 minutes to relax the gluten, which will make the dough more pliable.
- Meanwhile, prepare the filling. Using a skillet, cook the bacon over medium heat until most of the fat is rendered out. Remove the bacon and reserve. Drain off all but two tablespoons fat. Add the onion to the skillet and sauté over medium heat for 8 to10 minutes, stirring frequently, until browned. Increase heat to medium-high and add the sauerkraut. Cook, stirring frequently, for 10 to 15 minutes, until soft. Stir in the tomato paste, sugar, and broth. Reduce heat to low, then cover and simmer for 20 minutes. Remove from the heat and cool to room temperature before using to fill the vareniki
- Divide the dough in half and shape into two balls. Keep one ball covered with the towel. Using a rolling pin, roll dough out on a floured surface. Roll out very thin, about 1/16 inch thick, making sure it doesn't tear. Using a round cookie cutter or a drinking glass, cut

circles about 3 inches in diameter. Gather the scraps together into a ball and set aside; cover with a damp tea towel.

- In a large pot, bring 6 quarts of salted water to a boil.
- Meanwhile, assemble the vareniki. Place the bowl containing the egg whites within easy reach. Place 1 to 2 teaspoons of the filling in the middle of each circle, depending more or less on the size of the circle. Fold the dough over the filling to form a half-circle. Brush the edges with the egg white and press the edges firmly together with the tines of a fork to seal. As you assemble the vareniki, place them on a lightly floured large baking sheet about 1 inch apart and keep covered with a damp tea towel. When finished with the first batch, roll out the second ball of dough and make a second batch. Add the leftover scraps of dough to the scraps left from the first batch, knead into a ball, and roll out for a final batch.
- After water starts boiling, reduce the heat to medium. Carefully put half the vareniki into the water and boil for 7 to 9 minutes, stirring occasionally with a wooden spoon to prevent sticking, until they rise to the surface and are cooked through. Using a slotted spoon, carefully remove the vareniki and place them into a colander to drain thoroughly. Transfer to a deep serving bowl and toss with half the butter. Repeat for the second half of the vareniki. Use the reserved bacon as a topping. Serve with meat dish of your choice.
- Serves 8.

Reuben Stuffed Meatloaf

Meat
1 ½ pounds lean ground beef (can also use moose or elk)
1 cup soft breadcrumbs
½ cup sweet salad dressing (preferably Thousand Island)
1 medium egg
½ teaspoon salt
½ teaspoon black pepper
½ teaspoon caraway or dill seed
Reuben Filling
1 cup sauerkraut
½ cup corned beef, chopped
1 cup Swiss cheese, shredded

- Preheat oven to 350 degrees Fahrenheit.
- Combine meat mixture ingredients and mix well. Press half of the meat into the bottom of a casserole dish or loaf pan. Press the meat down in the center of the meatloaf, except the edges, making a small border.
- Combine filling ingredients and place over the meat layer, but not onto border. Top with remaining meat mixture, enclosing filling and sealing edges.
- Bake for 45 to 60 minutes, or until temperature on a meat thermometer reaches 145 degrees Fahrenheit. Let stand for 10 minutes before removing from pan. Serve with potatoes or rye bread.

White Beans with Sauerkraut and Smoked Ham

1 pound smoked ham, diced (ham can have a bit of fat)
1 14-ounce can white beans in tomato sauce
2 cups sauerkraut, thoroughly rinsed and drained
2 tablespoons lard or vegetable oil
1 medium onion, finely chopped
2 cloves garlic, grated
Freshly ground pepper, to taste
½ cup sour cream

- Place smoked ham, white beans, and sauerkraut into a lightly greased casserole dish.
- In a small frying pan, heat the lard or vegetable oil on medium-low. Add the onion and fry, stirring occasionally, till almost golden. Add onions and the garlic to casserole and mix all ingredients well.
- Put casserole into a preheated 350-degree Fahrenheit oven and cook for 35 to 45 minutes, until ham is cooked.
- Before serving, stir in the sour cream and mix well. Serve with a small salad. Serves 3 to 4.

Beans and Kraut Casserole

2 14-ounce cans baked beans
1 ½ cups brown sugar
2 tablespoons ketchup
2 cups sauerkraut, rinsed and drained
1 pound smoked polish or similar sausage, cut in 1-inch chunks

- Combine all ingredients in a greased 2 ½-quart casserole. Bake at 325 degrees Fahrenheit for about 2 hours.
- Serves 5 to 6.

Sauerkraut with Barbecued Pork Casserole

2 cups sauerkraut, drained
1 pound boneless pork sirloin (about 4 slices)
1 teaspoon garlic powder
Black pepper, to taste (optional)
¾ cup barbecue sauce

- Preheat oven to 350 degrees Fahrenheit.
- Spread sauerkraut evenly in a greased 11x7x1½-inch baking dish. Put pork in a skillet and brown both sides quickly. When browned, place pork on sauerkraut bed and sprinkle with garlic powder. Evenly spread barbecue sauce over pork. Cover with a lid or foil and bake at 350 degrees Fahrenheit for 45 to 60 minutes, until pork is cooked.
- Serve with potatoes of your choice and a salad.
- Serves 2 to 3.

Wieners and Kraut Casserole

1 pound wieners
4 cups sauerkraut
1 tablespoon caraway seeds
2 cups sour cream
1 tablespoon paprika

- Cut wieners into quarters and toss with sauerkraut. Mix in caraway seeds and put all into a greased casserole. Heat in a 400-degree Fahrenheit oven for 15 to 20 minutes.
- Stir in sour cream and sprinkle with paprika. Return to oven and broil to brown top lightly.
- Serves 6.

Sauerkraut Rice Casserole

2 tablespoons butter
1 medium onion, diced
4 cups sauerkraut, rinsed and drained
1 cup white rice
Salt and pepper to taste
Water

- In a small skillet, sauté onion in butter until tender.
- Put sauerkraut into a 2-quart casserole. Mix in rice and sautéed onion, salt, and pepper. Add water to just barely cover.
- Bake, uncovered, in a 350 degree Fahrenheit oven for 45 to 50 minutes.
- Serves 4.

Sauerkraut and Hamburger Casserole

1 small onion, chopped
2 tablespoons cooking oil
1 pound ground beef (can also use pork)
3 ½ cups sauerkraut, rinsed and drained
1 teaspoon caraway or dill seeds (optional)
1 cup cooked white or brown rice
1 14-ounce can stewed tomatoes

- Sauté onion in oil until soft. Add ground meat and brown lightly. Drain fat.
- Spread half the browned meat on the bottom of a casserole, then the sauerkraut. Sprinkle with caraway or dill seeds, if preferred. Spread the rice over top, then the remaining meat. Top evenly with stewed tomatoes.
- Bake at 350 degrees Fahrenheit for 45 to 60 minutes.
- Serves 6.

Turnip and Sauerkraut Casserole

4 average-sized turnips, sliced
1 ½ cups diced onion
2 teaspoons vegetable oil
4 cups sauerkraut, with a bit of juice
1 teaspoon caraway or dill seeds
¼ cup spicy brown mustard

- Cook or steam the turnips until tender-crisp. Drain.
- Using a skillet, sauté onions in the oil.
- Place sauerkraut on the bottom of a well-greased casserole dish and sprinkle with caraway seeds. Top with turnips and mustard, then the sautéed onions.
- Place in a 350 degree Fahrenheit oven and bake, uncovered, for 30 minutes. Stir casserole before serving.
- Serves 6.

Kraut Luncheon Casserole

2 tablespoons butter or bacon drippings
½ cup onion, sliced
7 cups sauerkraut
1 tart apple or medium-sized potato, peeled and grated
1 10-ounce can chicken broth, or same amount water
2 tablespoons brown sugar
1 teaspoon caraway or celery seeds

- Using an ovenproof (braising or roasting) pan, sauté onions in butter or bacon drippings on top of stove until clear. Add sauerkraut and sauté for 5 minutes. Add apple or potato, and chicken broth or water. Cook, uncovered, for 30 minutes.
- Add brown sugar and caraway or celery seeds. Cover, and continue cooking in a 350 degree Fahrenheit oven for 30 minutes longer.

Variation: Top sauerkraut with wieners, ham slices, or precooked sausages before putting casserole in the oven for the last 30 minutes.

Sauerkraut Filling for Perogies

2 cups very fine cut sauerkraut
1 medium onion, chopped
2 tablespoons cooking oil
1 ½ tablespoons sour cream
¼ teaspoon caraway or dill seed (or 1/8 teaspoon of each)
salt and pepper to taste
2 recipes perogy dough (Never Fail Perogy Dough)

- Measure out (without juice) 2 cups sauerkraut, place into a colander or large strainer. Run warm water over sauerkraut to rinse. Squeeze dry. Chop fine if sauerkraut is course.
- Sauté onion in until tender. Add sauerkraut and sour cream. Add caraway or dill seed and season to taste with salt and pepper.
- Cook over low heat for 10 minutes or until sauerkraut is tender and flavors are well blended. Do not fry. Chill thoroughly.
- Prepare perogy dough (see recipe below) and place 2 teaspoons filling on 3 ½-inch dough rounds.
- Assemble perogies; cook as you wish. Makes about 36 perogies.

Sauerkraut and Mushroom Filling for Perogies

1 ¾ cups drained sauerkraut, chopped very fine
1 tablespoon water
¼ cup chopped onion
1 cup mushrooms, chopped fine
2 teaspoons oil or butter
1/8 teaspoon pepper
1 hard-boiled egg, chopped
4 teaspoons sour cream
1 recipe perogy dough (See Never Fail Perogy Dough)

- Cook sauerkraut with 1 tablespoon water in a saucepan for 10 to 15 minutes.

- Sauté onion and mushrooms in butter. Add pepper and sauerkraut. Continue cooking for a minute, stirring to mix well. Add chopped egg and sour cream. Mix well.
- Variation: Instead of egg, use ¼ cup cooked and chopped sausage slices. Add the sausages when you add the pepper and sauerkraut to sautéed onions and mushrooms. This recipe will make 24 perogies (1 tablespoon filling per perogy).

Never Fail Perogy Dough

I call this my "Never Fail Dough" because of its work-ability and stick-ability, meaning that it won't come apart while cooking, something that some people making perogies for the first time, or even the first few times, have problems with. The reason for the stick-ability is because there is no oil in the dough, which, although it gives the dough certain softness, inhibits good sticking. Because of the milk content, however, the dough still retains a satisfying softness. I've also found that this dough makes especially attractive perogies, ones that won't lose their shape while cooking.

1 egg
¼ cup water
¼ cup milk
1 ¾ - 2 cups all-purpose white flour

- In a bowl, beat together egg, water, and milk, then slowly add flour, stirring first with a spoon, then kneading with lightly greased hands to make a soft dough. Knead for 5 minutes. Cover with a cloth and let rest for 15 minutes.
- Roll out the dough to 1/8-inch thickness. Cut out circles with a cup, drinking glass, or doughnut cutter. I have found that 3 ½-inch rounds are best.
- Place about 1 tablespoon filling in the center, fold over and seal edges. You may not need to brush edges with this dough to make them stick, but you certainly can if you choose to. Dough will make 18 to 24 perogies.

Cabbage and Sauerkraut Filling for Piróg or Pirozhkí
(Russian)

Note: *Piróg* is a large rectangular, square, or round pie that can be sweet or savory, depending on the filling. *Pirozhkí* are small filled oval pies. This is similar to the British pasty, which is a small half-moon shaped closed pie, usually containing some meat.

4 cups green cabbage
2 cups sauerkraut
3 tablespoons unsalted butter
3 tablespoons vegetable oil
4 hard-cooked eggs, finely chopped
Salt and black pepper to taste
2 tablespoons chopped fresh dill (optional)
1/3 cup plain dry breadcrumbs

I've included a classic filling (Cabbage and Sauerkraut) for either Piróg or Pirozhkí, two different kinds of pastry, along with instructions on how to assemble and bake these excellent Russian pies.

Yeast Dough for Piróg or Pirozhkí

This yeast dough is excellent for pieroghí (plural for Piróg) and pirozhkí.

1 package active dry yeast
2 teaspoons sugar or honey
2/3 cup lukewarm milk
1 cup unsalted butter
1 egg
½ teaspoon salt
3 ½ cups or slightly more white flour

- In a mixing bowl, combine the yeast, sugar or honey, and milk. Let stand for 5 minutes, until foamy. Add the butter, egg (lightly beaten), and salt to the yeast mixture. Mix well. Slowly add flour while stirring or beating. Knead dough for about 3 minutes. It should be smooth and rather loose. Shape into a ball, cover, and let stand for 10 minutes. You may also refrigerate it for up to 24 hours.
- This dough recipe will make 1 large piróg.

Sour Cream Pastry for Piróg or Pirozhkí

Here is an excellent pastry for piroghí (plural for piróg) and pirozhkí. This dough is very easy to make and has many applications. I have used this dough for regular items such as raisin pie and apple pie, but it is especially great for certain meat pies, including pasties (British cousin of the Russian meat-filled pirozhkí). The sour cream makes this great flaky short pastry pleasantly tart. For a sweet pie crust, add 2 tablespoons of sugar.

3 cups white flour
¾ teaspoon salt
½ teaspoon baking powder
1 cup plus 2 tablespoons unsalted butter
2 large egg yolks
2/3 cup sour cream

- In a large mixing bowl, combine the flour, salt, and baking powder. Add the butter and blend with a pastry blender or with your hands, until the flour resembles course crumbs.
- Mix together the egg yolks and sour cream, and slowly add to the flour mixture, working it into a pastry with your hands. Add a bit more flour if necessary.
- Place pastry onto a cool, lightly floured surface and knead just briefly, about 30 seconds. Divide the pastry into two balls, wrap them in plastic wrap and refrigerate for at least 1 hour. If you are using the pastry to make a piróg, form one part a bit larger than the other. This recipe will make about 45 pirozhkí or 1 piróg.

Piróg

1 recipe Cabbage and Sauerkraut Filling for Piróg
1 recipe Yeast Dough or Sour Cream Pastry
1 large egg yolk, beaten with 1 teaspoon milk

- Blanche the cabbage in boiling salted water for 3 minutes. Drain well and squeeze the cabbage to remove any excess liquid. And well-drained sauerkraut and mix well. Heat the butter and oil in a wok or large skillet over medium heat. Add the cabbage and cook, stirring, until soft and colored, 15 to 20 minutes. Remove from the heat and stir in eggs, spices and dill. For extra flavor you may also add a bit of Hungarian paprika. Cool filling to room temperature.
- Preheat oven to 350 to 375 degrees Fahrenheit.
- Lightly butter an 18x12x1-inch baking sheet. Divide the dough into 2 slightly uneven pieces. Roll out the larger piece of dough to 14x10 inches. Drape it over the rolling pin and transfer it to the baking sheet. Sprinkle the bread crumbs over the dough surface, then spread the filling evenly over the crumbs, leaving a 1 ½-inch border all around. Roll out the second piece of dough to 12½x8½ inches. Place over the filling, fold the edges of the bottom crust, and press to seal. Crimp edges with the tines of a fork. Brush the top with the egg wash. If you are using the yeast dough, allow it to rest for 20 minutes before baking.
- Bake the piróg in the middle of the oven until the crust is golden and baked through. Bake about 45 minutes. If crust is browning too quickly, cover loosely with aluminum foil.
- Cut the piróg into 3-inch squares before serving. Serve warm. One large piróg serves 8 to10.

Pirozhkí

(Russian)

1 recipe Cabbage and Sauerkraut Filling for Piróg
1 recipe Yeast Dough or Sour Cream Pastry
1 large egg yolk, beaten with 1 teaspoon milk

- Pirozhkí are small filled oval-shaped pastries. They are ideal finger foods or accompaniments for soups.
- Preheat the oven to 350 degrees Fahrenheit. Lightly butter two large baking sheets. Divide the dough into 4 pieces. Wrap in plastic wrap and refrigerate those you're not working with right away.
- Roll one piece out to a thickness of about 1/8 inch. Cut 3-inch rounds with a cookie cutter or drinking glass. Flatten each round slightly between your fingers and place 1 to 2 teaspoons of the filling (the amount will determine the size and number of pirozhkí you'll end up with). Fold the edges up so they meet the center and press together firmly to seal. Pat the pirozhók into an oval shape. Place it on a lightly oiled baking sheet, seam side down. Repeat with remaining dough and filling, placing the pirozhkí 1 inch apart. Gather the leftover scraps of dough, press into a ball, reroll, and use. If not all the pirozhkí fit on two baking sheets, bake them in batches, keeping the unbaked ones refrigerated.
- Brush pirozhkí with the egg wash and bake, with the rack situated in the middle of the oven, until golden brown, 25 to 30 minutes. Serve warm. Makes 45 to 50 pirozhkí.

Kraut Burritos

1 pound lean ground beef, pork, or chicken
1 cup cooked dried beans, drained (can use one kind or a mixture of several)
2 tablespoons olive oil
1 cup chopped onion
½ cup finely chopped fresh mushrooms
1 large tomato, chopped
2 cups sauerkraut, drained
1 teaspoon salt
1 ½ - 2 tablespoons Cajun seasoning, or to taste
1 cup shredded cheddar or mozzarella cheese
½ cup sour cream
12 8-inch wheat tortillas

- Brown the meat well in a large skillet. Drain off fat and transfer browned meat to a bowl; set aside.
- Add oil to skillet and heat over low to medium heat. Add onions and mushrooms; cook until onions are a soft, about 5 minutes. Add chopped tomato, sauerkraut, beans, and Cajun seasoning. Cook for 5 minutes, mashing some of the beans with a fork. Add browned beef and cook, stirring to blend, for 7 to 10 minutes, until meat is cooked through. Stir while cooking, adding a bit of water if mixture gets too dry. Take off heat; stir in cheese and sour cream.
- Place about ¾ cup filling across the center of a tortilla, leaving about an inch on each side uncovered. Fold sides over filling and roll up tortilla. Repeat with remaining tortillas and filling ingredients. Serve immediately. If not serving immediately, refrigerate or freeze burritos. Heat in microwave before serving.
- Makes 12 burritos.

Kraut Carrot Burritos

4 medium carrots
1 cup bean sprouts
½ tablespoon olive oil
1 cup sauerkraut, rinsed and drained
2 tablespoons pimientos (optional)
1 cup shredded mozzarella, cheddar, or similar cheese
1 tablespoon prepared mustard
½ cup sour cream
¼ teaspoon paprika
1/8 teaspoon cayenne pepper
4 whole wheat tortillas

- Peel and chop carrots; steam-cook until soft.
- Sauté sprouts lightly in olive oil for 2 minutes over medium heat. Stir in sauerkraut and pimientos; heat through. Add carrots and remaining filling ingredients; mix well.
- Place equal amounts of filling on each of the tortilla; tuck in the ends and roll. Serves 4.

Kraut Sloppy Joes

1 pound lean ground beef
1 medium onion, chopped
1 ½ cups sauerkraut, rinsed and drained
1 teaspoon basil
½ teaspoon caraway seeds
1 10-ounce can tomato sauce
Hamburger buns

- Put ground beef and onions into a large skillet. Cook over medium heat until beef is well browned. Drain fat.
- Reduce heat to low; stir in sauerkraut, basil, caraway seeds, and tomato sauce. Simmer for 20 to 30 minutes, until meat is well cooked. Serve on open hamburger buns.

Krauted Stuffings, Toppings, Sauces, and Dips

Savory Sauerkraut Stuffing

¼ cup butter
1 cup finely chopped celery
1 cup diced red onion
1 teaspoon thyme or rosemary
1 pound sauerkraut, rinsed and squeezed dry
1 cup chicken broth
1 cup cooked ham, diced
½ cup pitted, chopped black olives
1/3 cup chopped and lightly toasted walnuts
¾ cup chopped fresh parsley
4 cups stale white bread, cut in ½-inch cubes
¼ teaspoon black pepper

- In a large skillet, melt butter. Add the celery, onions, and thyme or rosemary; sauté over medium heat for 5 to 7 minutes, until onion and celery are tender. Stir in sauerkraut and cook 5 minutes more. Add broth and simmer 10 minutes.
- Combine sauerkraut mixture with all remaining ingredients; mixing thoroughly to ensure that bread is completely coated and moistened.
- Stuff bird. Depending on the size of the bird you may have some stuffing left, which you may bake outside of the bird, or bake all of it like that. If so, sprinkle an extra ¼ to ½ cup of chicken broth on top and cover the casserole or baking dish with foil. Bake at 350 degrees Fahrenheit for 30 minutes. Uncover and bake another 15 minutes to brown.
- This recipe makes 8 cups stuffing. Typically, that amount is about right for 1 turkey, 2 roasting chickens, 1 goose, or 2 ducks.

Apple Sauerkraut Stuffing

You can use this excellent stuffing for chicken or turkey. The ingredients and recipe below are for a 2 ½ to 3-pound chicken, which is likely the smallest bird you'll roast. If the bird is 5 to 6 pounds, double the stuffing ingredients, if 7 to 9 pounds, triple it, if 10 to 12 pounds, multiply the stuffing ingredients by 4, if 12 to 15 pounds, multiply by 5, and so on up.

1 cup sauerkraut, for stuffing (don't rinse)
¼ cup grated apple (preferably sweet)
¼ cup dried white bread crumbs
½ teaspoon caraway seed
1/8 teaspoon black pepper
1/8 teaspoon paprika (optional)
¼ cup sauerkraut, some paprika, salt, and black pepper

- Mix all ingredients except the ones given on the last line of the above list. Place bird in a roasting pan. Stuff bird with stuffing mixture. Rub remaining sauerkraut and spices all over bird. Pour a bit of water into the pan, about 1/8 inch deep. Preheat oven to 425 degrees Fahrenheit and roast the bird at this high temperature for 10 to 20 minutes, depending on the size of bird. Reduce heat and continue roasting at 325 to 350 degrees Fahrenheit. Follow standard procedures of baking chicken or turkey as shown in any major cookbook.
- It is very important to baste the bird a few times, so that the sauerkraut flavor and the juices from the bird saturate the meat. The result will be that the meat will have a subtle and very satisfying kraut flavor when done. A 2 ½ to 3-pound bird will take 1 to 1 ½ hours to cook. You can tell if the bird is done by wriggling the drumstick. When done, it will be quite soft, so that you can easily pull it from the bird.
- Some basic roasting times for larger chicken or turkey when roasting the bird at 325 to 350 degrees Fahrenheit:

6 to 8 pounds: 3 to 3 ½ hours
8 to 10 pounds: 3 ½ to 3 ¾ hours
10 to 12 pounds: 3 ¾ to 4 hours
12 to 14 pounds: 4 to 4 ¼ hours
14 to 16 pounds: 4 ¼ to 4 ½ hours
16 to 18 pounds: 4 ½ to 4 ¾ hours

Sauerkraut and Rye Bread Stuffing for Thanksgiving Turkey

½ pound country-style bacon, cut in ½ -inch pieces
2 cups chopped onion
1 ½ cups chopped celery, including leaves
1 ½ cups chopped carrots
1 tablespoon chopped fresh thyme
1 teaspoon caraway seeds, crushed
1 teaspoon celery seeds
2 teaspoons salt
½ cup dry white wine
2 small tart apples, peeled and chopped
8 cups lightly toasted ½-inch rye bread cubes
3 cups sauerkraut, lightly rinsed and drained
Freshly ground black pepper to taste

- Using a large skillet, cook the bacon over medium-high heat until crisp. Remove from pan and put in a large mixing bowl; set aside.
- Pour off all but 3 or 4 tablespoons of the bacon grease from the skillet. Add onion, celery, carrots, thyme, caraway seeds, celery seeds, and salt. Cook over medium heat for about 10 minutes, until vegetables are a bit soft. Add the wine and bring to a boil, stirring while heating. Mix in the apples and cook, covered, until the apples are soft.
- Remove from heat and combine bacon, bread cubes, and sauerkraut in the large mixing bowl. Season with pepper; toss to mix well.
- Stuff the turkey in the usual way, but don't overstuff the bird. If you have some stuffing left, you can bake it by putting it into a casserole; pour a cup or two of stock over the stuffing and bake it, covered, for about 45 minutes at 350 degrees Fahrenheit, until heated through.
- Makes 12 to 14 cups of stuffing.

Sauerkraut Relish

1 cup sauerkraut, drained and chopped
½ cup minced celery
½ cup finely chopped olives
2 tablespoons finely chopped pimientos
½ cup grated carrots
½ cup minced dill pickles
¼ cup clear honey

- In a bowl, combine all ingredients; mix well. Cover bowl with plastic wrap and refrigerate for 8 to 10 hours to blend.

Sauerkraut Relish

1 cup finely chopped onion
3 cups finely chopped celery
1 ½ cups finely chopped green pepper
1 ½ cups finely chopped red pepper
3 ½ cups sauerkraut, drained
About 1 cup sugar (to taste)
½ cup olive oil
½ cup lemon juice

- In a bowl, mix together all ingredients except the last three.
- In small bowl combine sugar oil and vinegar; stir to dissolve sugar. Pour over vegetables and mix well.
- Refrigerate for at least 1 hour before serving.

Sweet and Sour Slaw

1 ½ cups sugar
¼ cup vegetable oil
½ cup apple cider vinegar
4 cups Sauerkraut, drained
1 cup chopped onion
½ cup chopped celery
¾ cup finely chopped green pepper
¾ cup finely chopped red pepper
¾ cup finely chopped yellow pepper
1 teaspoon mustard seeds
1 teaspoon celery seeds

- Combine all ingredients and toss to mix well. Cover and refrigerate 6 to 8 hours.
- Serve as a side dish or topping for barbecued pork sandwiches. Serves about 15.

Sauerkraut Topping for Hot-dogs

3 ½ cups sauerkraut, rinsed and drained
½ cup sweet pickle relish
¼ cup brown sugar
2 tablespoons prepared mustard
1 teaspoon caraway seeds

- Mix all ingredients in a saucepan and cook over low heat until heated through.
- Serve with hot dogs. Makes four servings.

Spinach-Apple Curried Spread

10 ounces spinach
½ cup mayonnaise
1 teaspoon curry powder
1 small apple, unpeeled, finely diced
1/3 cup peanuts, chopped
½ cup mellow flavored chutney
1 cup sauerkraut, with juice

- Wash spinach and drain it well using a salad spin-dryer. If fresh spinach is not available, use 1 10-ounce package of frozen spinach; squeeze out juice. Finely chop spinach and mix with mayonnaise and curry.
- Add apple, peanuts, chutney, and sauerkraut.
- Mix well with a spoon and refrigerate.

Kraut and Sour Cream Topping for Baked Potato

¼ cup sauerkraut, finely chopped
¼ cup sour cream
½ teaspoon dill weed
2 teaspoons bacon bits

- Combine all ingredients except bacon bits.
- Place a dollop of topping mixture on baked potatoes, then sprinkle with bacon.
- Serve with meat dish of your choice and salad.

Sauerkraut Topping for Burgers and Sandwiches

4 cups sauerkraut, rinsed and thoroughly drained
1 large sweet Spanish onion, sliced
4 tablespoons butter
¼ cup brown sugar
¼ cup ketchup
Seasoning salt, to taste
3 tablespoons Worcestershire sauce

- Rinse and drain sauerkraut.
- Sauté sliced onion in butter until soft. Add sauerkraut and cook, stirring, until lightly browned. Stir in remaining ingredients and cook over low heat for 10 to 15 minutes, until well blended.
- Transfer topping to a bowl and refrigerate for at least 2 hours.

Krauted Salsa

1 14-ounce can black beans, drained and rinsed
2/3 cup sauerkraut, rinsed, drained, and chopped
1/3 cup chopped fresh cilantro
1 4-ounce can green chilies, chopped
2 tablespoons lemon or lime juice
2 large tomatoes, peeled, seeded and chopped
¼ cup finely chopped green onions

- Combine all ingredients in a mixing bowl; mix well.
- Cover and refrigerate for 2 or more hours before serving.
- Makes about 3 cups.

Sauerkraut Sauce

2 cups sauerkraut, rinsed and liquid squeezed out
1 cup chicken broth or water
1 tablespoon sugar
Apple cider vinegar to taste (optional)
Salt to taste
1 tablespoon butter, melted
1 tablespoon flour

- Put sauerkraut and broth in a small saucepan and cook over low heat for 1 to 1 ½ hours.
- Add sugar, apple cider vinegar if preferred, and salt. Bring to boil.
- Mix butter with flour; add to sauce and, while stirring, bring to boil. Serve with fried foods.

Sauerkraut Sauce

4 cups sauerkraut, rinsed and drained (reserve 1 to 1 ½ cups liquid)
½ cup butter
1 medium onion, chopped
Salt and pepper to taste
2 tablespoons lemon juice
1 tablespoon honey

- Puree sauerkraut in a food processor, then braise in ¼ cup butter. Sauté onion in remaining butter and add to sauerkraut. Add 1 cup sauerkraut juice, cover, and stew for 30 minutes, adding more juice as needed to make a medium thick sauce. Add salt and pepper, lemon juice, and honey for a sweet and sour taste.
- Serve with roast goose or duck.

Sweet and Sour Sauce for Burgers

2 cups sauerkraut, drained and chopped
1 cup whole berry cranberry sauce
1/3 cup chili sauce
1 teaspoon Worcestershire sauce
½ cup water
5 tablespoons brown sugar

- Taste sauerkraut for sourness, as some brands may require light rinsing if too sour. Combine ingredients in a skillet or saucepan and simmer over low heat for 20 minutes. Top burgers with sauce.

Cocktail Kraut Dip

¼ cup seafood cocktail sauce
½ package onion soup mix
½ cup sauerkraut, rinsed, drained and finely chopped
1 4-ounce package cream cheese

- Mix all ingredients and chill before serving. Serve with seafood, crackers, or chips.

Dill and Sauerkraut Dip

1 envelope onion soup mix
3 ½ cups sauerkraut, drained and chopped
2 cups sour cream
1 teaspoon dried dill weed
½ cup bacon bits

- Mix all ingredients together and chill before serving.

Blushing Sauerkraut Dip

1 4-ounce package cream cheese
½ package onion soup mix
2/3 cup sauerkraut, drained
½ cup chili sauce

- Blend all ingredients together and chill before serving.

Kraut Cheese Dip

2 2/3 cups melted process cheese (1 pound)
1 ¼ cups sauerkraut, undrained, finely chopped
1 ½ tablespoons minced onion
1 ½ tablespoons minced red pepper
4 teaspoons ketchup
2 teaspoons fresh dill weed (optional)

- Melt the cheese in a double boiler or in the microwave. Add remaining ingredients and stir to mix thoroughly.
- Serves about 8.

Kraut Desserts

Beer and Sauerkraut Fudge Cake

¾ cup butter
1 ½ cups sugar
3 eggs
1 teaspoon vanilla
½ cup cocoa
2 ¼ cups sifted white flour
1 teaspoon baking powder
1 teaspoon baking soda
¼ teaspoon salt
1 to 1 ¼ cups beer
¾ cup sauerkraut, drained and finely chopped
½ cup each of raisins and walnuts (optional)

- Preheat the oven to 350 degrees Fahrenheit.
- In a large mixing bowl, cream butter and sugar. Beat in the eggs, then and add vanilla. Beat well. Combine dry ingredients and add to creamed mixture alternately with beer, ending with dry ingredients. Stir in Sauerkraut. Pour into a 9x13-inch glass baking dish or cake pan and bake at 350 degrees Fahrenheit for 35 to 40 minutes. Cool cake and frost as desired.
- Yields 1 9x13-inch cake.

Sauerkraut Apple Cake

Cake
2 cups white flour
2 teaspoons baking powder
2 teaspoons cinnamon
1 teaspoon baking soda
1 teaspoon salt
½ teaspoon nutmeg
1 cup white sugar
½ cup yellow sugar, packed
4 eggs
1 teaspoon vanilla (optional)
1 cup vegetable oil
2 cups sauerkraut, rinsed and juice squeezed out
1 large sweet apple, peeled, cored, and chopped
1 cup chopped walnuts or pecans

Frosting
1 8-ounce package cream cheese, softened
½ cup unsalted butter, softened
4 cups icing sugar
1 teaspoon vanilla
2 teaspoons cinnamon
1 tablespoon grated orange zest
1/8 teaspoon salt

Cake
- In a large mixing bowl, whisk together flour, baking powder, cinnamon, baking soda, salt, and nutmeg. Set aside.
- Preheat the oven to 325 degrees Fahrenheit.
- In another mixing bowl, combine the sugars. While beating with a whisk, add the eggs and then the oil; blend well. Stir in the sauerkraut, apple, and nuts.
- Add the dry ingredients and stir lightly, until just moistened. Pour into a lightly greased 9x13-inch glass baking dish and bake for 35 minutes, or until a knife inserted in the center

comes out clean and the cake's edges are just beginning to pull away from the pan. Set aside and allow to cool before adding the frosting.

Frosting

- In a large mixing bowl, beat the cream cheese and butter until well blended. Add the icing sugar gradually, then the vanilla, cinnamon, orange zest, and salt. Beat until smooth. Spread icing on cake, and serve. You can make icing ahead of time, in which case it's best to refrigerate cake before serving, or make icing and spread on cake just before serving.
- Yields 1 9x13-inch cake.

Kraut Chocolate Kuchen

2 ½ cups flour
1 teaspoon baking soda
1 teaspoon baking powder
1 ½ cups white sugar
2/3 cups shortening
3 medium eggs
1 ½ teaspoons vanilla
½ cup cocoa
¼ teaspoon salt
1 cup water
1 cup sauerkraut, rinsed and drained
1 19-ounce can cherry or blueberry pie filling
Shredded coconut (optional)

- Preheat oven to 375 degrees Fahrenheit.
- In a small mixing bowl, sift together flour, baking soda, and baking powder. Set aside.
- In a large mixing bowl, cream sugar and shortening. Add eggs, vanilla, cocoa, and salt; mix well. Alternately add flour and water. Add sauerkraut and mix well.
- Put batter into a greased and floured baking pan and bake for 45 to 50 minutes.
- Spread cherry pie filling over the top of cake. Sprinkle with coconut if preferred.
- Serves 10.

Sauerkraut Puff-Pie

Dough
3/4 pound suet fat or soft butter
2 cups flour
1 egg
2 tablespoons water
Pinch of salt
Filling
1 ½ pounds cooked sauerkraut, with no liquid
1 pound wieners or bacon, chopped and lightly fried
1 cup light cream
3 tablespoons tomato sauce
1 tablespoon paprika
1 egg yolk

- Melt suet and work it into all other dough ingredients to make a smooth firm dough. If using butter, follow same instructions except for melting butter. There's no need to melt it, but it should be quite soft.
- Grease a baking dish and line it with two-thirds of the dough. Arrange sauerkraut and wieners or bacon in alternate layers. Mix cream, tomato sauce, and paprika; pour evenly over sauerkraut and wieners. Roll out remaining dough to fit across top of pie and prick with fork or knife to provide air holes for steam escape. You may also cut dough strips and lay them on top in any desired pattern. Brush top dough with egg yolk. Bake at 350 degrees Fahrenheit for about 1 hour.

Sauerkraut Chocolate Cake

Cake
½ cup butter, softened
1 ½ cups white sugar
3 eggs
1 teaspoon vanilla
2 cups white flour
½ cup cocoa
1 teaspoon baking powder
1 teaspoon baking soda
½ teaspoon salt
1 - 1 ¼ cups water
1 cup sauerkraut, drained and chopped
Frosting
1 ¼ cups butter, softened
4 1-ounce squares unsweetened chocolate
5 cups icing sugar
1/3 cup milk

- In a mixing bowl, cream the butter and sugar. While beating, add the eggs and vanilla.
- Combine the dry ingredients and add to the creamed mixture alternately with water. Stir in sauerkraut.
- Pour equal amounts of the batter into 2 greased and floured 8-inch cake pans. Bake at 350 degrees Fahrenheit for 30 to 35 minutes or until a knife inserted near the center comes out clean.
- Cool in pans for 10 minutes before removing to a wire rack to cool completely.
- To make frosting, beat butter, chocolate, and vanilla in a mixing bowl. Add icing sugar and beat. Add milk and beat until smooth and fluffy.
- Place one of the cakes on a serving plate. Spread some icing evenly over top: about ¼ inch, then lay the other cake on top. Spread icing over the top and the sides of cake.
- Serves 12.

Sauerkraut Custard Pie

¾ cup cream-milk
1 ½ cups drained and finely chopped sauerkraut
½ cup white sugar
3 eggs
1 teaspoon vanilla extract
1 9-inch pie shell

- Preheat oven to 425 degrees Fahrenheit.
- In a large bowl, mix cream-milk, sauerkraut, sugar, eggs, and vanilla.
- Pour mixture into pie shell. Bake at 425 degrees Fahrenheit for 10 minutes, then reduce heat to 350 degrees Fahrenheit and continue baking for 20 minutes or until a knife inserted into filling an inch from the edge comes out clean.
- This recipe will make one 9-inch pie. If you wish to make more than one pie, the calculations are easy. Simply multiply the ingredients by the number of pies you wish to make.

Reuben Cheesecake

1 ½ cups whole grain rye or fine wheat cracker crumbs
½ cup melted butter
16 ounces cream cheese, softened
4 eggs
¼ cup all-purpose white flour
2/3 cup Thousand Island dressing
1 ¼ cups shredded Swiss cheese
1 cup sauerkraut, rinsed, well drained, and chopped
½ pound corned beef, shredded (may also use cooked ham)

- Combine cracker crumbs and butter; press onto the bottom and 1 inch up the sides of a 9-inch spring-form pan. Set aside.

- Using an electric beater, beat cream cheese at high speed until light and fluffy; add eggs, one at a time, and beat until well blended. Add flour and salad dressing, and continue beating until blended. Fold in Swiss cheese and remaining ingredients.
- Pour cheese mixture into the pan and spread out evenly.
- Place pan in a 300 degree Fahrenheit oven and bake for about 50 to 60 minutes or until set. Turn oven off, partially open oven door; and let cheesecake sit in oven for 1 hour. Remove from oven, and let cool completely on a wire rack. Cover with plastic wrap and put in refrigerator to chill through.

Kraut Stuffed Apples

6 apples (depending on size)
3 ½ cups sauerkraut, rinsed and drained
¼ cup chopped walnuts
¼ cup chopped raisins
¼ cup brown sugar
Sugar, cinnamon, or graham cracker crumbs
Sour cream

- Wash apples and core to leave a good cavity. Peel skin ½ inch down from the top.
- Mix sauerkraut, walnuts, raisins, and ¼ cup brown sugar. Fill apple cavities with mixture.
- Place in a buttered casserole and sprinkle tops with sugar, cinnamon, or graham cracker crumbs. Top each apple with a dollop of sour cream.
- Bake at 350 degrees Fahrenheit for 30 to 35 minutes, or until tender.

Kraut Drinks

Bloody Mary with Sauerkraut Juice

8 ounces of your favorite bloody Mary mix
1 cup ice
1 tablespoon sauerkraut juice
1 slice lime or celery stalk, for garnish

- Pour bloody Mary mix over ice.
- Add sauerkraut juice.
- Add slice of lime or celery stalk.

Holiday Drink

1 48-ounce can tomato juice
45 ounces sauerkraut juice
1 large onion

- Pour juices into a punch bowl; stir to mix.
- Peel and quarter onion; add to juice.
- Cover with plastic wrap; refrigerate overnight or at least 8 hours.
- Serve with Thanksgiving or Christmas dinner.
- Makes 12 drinks.

Tomato Sauerkraut Cocktail

2 parts tomato juice
1 part sauerkraut juice
Dash of Worcestershire sauce
Pinch of horseradish
A few drops of lemon juice

- Mix ingredients together and chill before serving.

Recipe Index

Sauerkraut Breads – 33

Krauted Appetizers – 39

Sauerkraut Soups, Borschts, and Stews – 49

Sauerkraut Salads –75

Krauted Sandwiches, Dogs, and Burgers – 83

Bavarian Beef Patties with Sauerkraut –146
Bavarian Sauerkraut Rolls –168
Beans and Kraut Casserole –173
Beef Brisket with Sauerkraut –128
Beef Brisket with Sauerkraut and Applesauce –128
Beer Braised Sauerkraut with Sausages –133
Bierocks (Bread rolls with zesty meat and sauerkraut stuffing) **–144**
Braised Pork Chops with Sauerkraut # 1 – 116
Braised Pork Chops with Sauerkraut # 2 –116
Cabbage and Sauerkraut Filling for Piróg or Pirozhkí (Russian)**–180**
Cabbage Rolls Stuffed with Sauerkraut (Ukrainian)**–163**
Chicken and Bratwurst with Sauerkraut –158
Chicken Cooked in Sauerkraut –154
Chicken in the Pot –147
Chicken Meatball Kraut Skillet – 157
Chicken Sauerkraut Bake –156
Chicken Thighs with Sauerkraut –154
Chicken with Sauerkraut –155
Choucroute Garni (Alsatian Cured Meats with Sauerkraut) **–130**
Crockpot Chicken and Sauerkraut –155
Crockpot Chicken Reuben –153
Crockpot Sweet and Sour Kraut with Pork Chops –117
Danish Pork Roast and Sauerkraut in Beer –118
Farmer Sausages with Sauerkraut –132
Fish with Sauerkraut –160
Greek-Style Chicken with Sauerkraut –148
Kraut Burritos –184
Kraut Carrot Burritos –185
Kraut Chicken Parmesan –152
Krauted Chicken Pie –151
Krauted Pork Kabobs –119
Krauted Wild Duck –160
Kraut Luncheon Casserole –177
Kraut Sloppy Joes –185
Kraut Stuffed Green Peppers –145

Krauted Stuffings, Toppings, Sauces, and Dips –187

Krauted Desserts – 197

Beer and Sauerkraut Fudge Cake –197
Kraut Chocolate Kuchen –199
Kraut Stuffed Apples – 203
Reuben Cheesecake – 202
Sauerkraut Apple Cake –198
Sauerkraut Chocolate Cake – 201
Sauerkraut Custard Pie – 202
Sauerkraut Puff-Pie – 200

Krauted Drinks – 205

Bloody Mary with Sauerkraut Juice – 205
Holiday Drink – 205
Tomato Sauerkraut Cocktail – 206

Bibliography

Kaufmann, Klaus, and Schöneck, Annelies. *The Cultured Cabbage: Rediscovering the Art of Making Sauerkraut*. Burnaby, British Columbia: *alive* books, 1997.

Pitchford, Paul. *Healing With Whole Food: Oriental Traditions and Modern Medicine*. Berkeley, California: North Atlantic Books, 1993.

Home Canning. Alberta Agriculture, 1983.

About the Author

Samuel Hofer is a widely known author of several books. His previous cookbooks were *The Hutterite Treasury of Recipes* (1986), *Soups and Borschts* (1988), *The Hutterite Community Cookbook* (1992), *A feast of Perogies and Dumplings* (1998), *and A Treasury of Soups, Borschts, Stews and Chowders* (1999). He is also known for his fiction and non-fiction writing, including the classic *Born Hutterite* (1991), a novel, *Dance like a Poor Man* (1995), and *The Hutterites: Lives and Images of a Communal People* (1998). He lives in Saskatoon, Saskatchewan.